Wanda Luttrell

Chariot Books is an imprint of Chariot Victor Publishing
Cook Communications, Colorado Springs, CO 80918
Cook Communications, Paris, Ontario
Kingsway Communications, Eastbourne, England

Cover design by Mary Schluchter, Andrea Boven
Cover illustration by Bill Farnsworth
Interior illustrations by Guy Wolek
First printing, 1997
Printed in the United States of America
01 5 4 3

Sarah felt a shiver travel down her own spine, as Pa cocked his gun. She was glad he had carried it with him this morning.

"Della, you and the young ones take shelter there behind the woodpile," Pa ordered. "I wish Luke had come on home with us instead of gallivanting off to the Larkins' for Sunday dinner!" Sarah heard him mutter as he walked quietly toward the cabin.

She peered over the stacked wood, as Pa slowly pushed open the cabin door and disappeared inside. "May the good Lord have mercy upon us!" Sarah heard him exclaim. Then he called, "Della, come here, quick!"

Be sure to read all the books
in Sarah's Journey

Home on Stoney Creek
Stranger in Williamsburg
Reunion in Kentucky
Whispers in Williamsburg
Shadows on Stoney Creek

Also Available as an Audio Book:
Home on Stoney Creek

Contents

For my mother, Odette Lusby Pardi,
who will always have her own
unique place in my heart.

N
Ohio River
Kentucky River
Stoney Creek
Salt River
Fort Harrod
Logans Fort
Fort Boonesborough
Sandy River
River
Cumberland
Kentucky
circa 1775

1

Sarah Moore stood in the cabin doorway, listening to the creek running over the rocks beyond the meadow. A thick white mist hung low over the water and stretched wispy fingers into the meadow, as though reaching for a bouquet of wild asters. "Farewell to Summer" Ma called the little flowers that spread a purple haze over the meadows and hillsides, for summer was ending and autumn frosts would soon come to kill the less hardy blooming plants.

It had been near dark when Sarah and Pa had ridden into the yard last evening, and she hadn't had a good look at the homestead her family had rebuilt after the Indians had burned the first one.

Sarah took a deep breath of the mellow, leaf-scented air. It felt good to be home this crisp October morning, back on the banks of Stoney Creek, with Pa's snug, new two-story cabin behind her, Ma busy churning a new batch of butter over by the fireplace, Jamie playing with his corncob farm near the hearth, and little Elizabeth still asleep in the big bed in the next room.

"A mist like that always makes me uneasy," Ma said from

the doorway behind her, "especially with your pa and Luke likely to be gone all day."

Sarah's brother and father had left an hour ago to cut wood at the edge of the forest that surrounded the cabin on three sides. A long rick of cut logs already stretched along the rail fence between the yard and the barn lot, but Pa had built fireplaces in both of the new cabin's downstairs rooms, and it would take a lot of wood to keep them going through even a mild winter.

"It's just a little fog rising off the creek, Ma," Sarah reassured her. "The sun will burn it away in an hour or two."

"But you just never know what a mist like that is hiding," Ma said. "Strange things have been going on around here the last couple of weeks."

★ Chapter One ★

"What kind of strange things, Ma?"

"Folks have been missing things, food mostly. But Mrs. Larkin had a cover stolen right off her clothes pole where she was airing it, and the Mackeys lost a bearskin from where it had been drying out in their barn."

"Could it be Indians?" Sarah asked.

Ma shook her head. "Nobody knows. But the dogs don't growl like they usually do when Indians are around."

Sarah looked down toward the creek where the mist swirled and eddied. She hoped it hid no more than a familiar, friendly creek and a bank covered with wildflowers! She shivered.

"I don't mean to frighten you, Sarah," Ma said, "but I don't want you taking chances. You've been living in a civilized town away from the wilderness for a long time."

"I haven't forgotten how it is out here, Ma," she said. "I'll just have to get used to it again."

"Will you miss Williamsburg terribly, Sarah?" Ma asked then.

A quick pang of longing for the excitement and culture of Virginia's capital city ran through Sarah. Then she looked back at the sturdy cabin Pa had built. She turned to look at the dark forest that surrounded them on three sides. Who knew what dangers lurked there—bears and other wild animals certainly, and possibly, Indians seeking to destroy their home and kill them or run them out of Kentucky. But the golden sun was spilling over the hilltop and onto the trees, its fiery light burning away the mist and kindling the red oaks and orange maples until they seemed ablaze with color.

Sarah turned to smile at Ma. "Yes, I'll miss it," she said honestly, "but with the capital being moved to Richmond and Aunt Charity and Uncle Ethan moving their family with it, Williamsburg wouldn't be the same to me. And with Pa right there in town to seek protection from the legislature for the Kentucky settlements, it just seemed logical that I should come home with him, while I had the chance."

"I'm sure you'll miss your cousins," Ma said. "You must have enjoyed being in a household with girls so near your own age. I remember what good times Charity and Rose and I had growing up together."

"Abigail and Tabitha and I shared some good times," Sarah admitted, "but Tabby's all wrapped up in her plans to marry Seth Coler, and 'Gail's all wrapped up in 'Gail. It's little Meggie I truly will miss. She has become like a little sister to me. We even shared a room, and a big soft bed under the eaves, with a big old cedar tree outside the window that whispered and moaned us to sleep."

Ma laughed. "I realize that sharing a bed with a two-year-old sister, and with a rowdy five-year-old brother in the trundle bed beside you, won't be quite the same. I hope you don't mind sharing with them, Sarah," she said. "I put you all in the room Pa built for him and me because it allows me to work in the big room without waking the children early in the morning or late at night. When Jamie's a little older, I'll let him move upstairs with Luke."

"I don't mind, Ma," Sarah said.

"By the way, how old is Megan now?" Ma asked. "I haven't seen any of my nieces for so long, I doubt I'd recognize them!"

"She's nearly nine, going on twenty-nine!" Sarah laughed, feeling a great longing to see Meggie again, but it seemed that all good things must end sooner or later, or there would be no little purple flowers called "Farewell to Summer."

"I think I'll go pick a bouquet for the dinner table, Ma," she said, "if you don't need me for a few minutes."

Jamie looked up from his corncobs. "I'm not going, Sarah,"

he said seriously, as though she had invited him along. "I've got to finish this fence before my cows get out."

Sarah hid a grin. Jamie's "cows" were fat pine cones he had gathered at the edge of the forest. "I suppose a man's work has to be done," she agreed.

Little Elizabeth toddled into the room in her long nightgown, rubbing the sleep out of her deep blue eyes that were partially hidden under uncombed, corn silk yellow bangs.

"You want to go pick flowers, Elizabeth?" Sarah asked.

The baby stared at her warily, then looked at Ma.

"It's all right, Elizabeth," Ma said. "You can go with your big sister if you want to."

Elizabeth looked back at Sarah uncertainly.

"She doesn't remember me, Ma," Sarah said sadly. "She doesn't remember the hours I spent taking care of her last year when you and she were so sick. I might as well never have been there!"

Ma smiled. "Honey, if you hadn't taken such good care of us, Elizabeth and I might not be here now."

"Oh, Ma, it was Malinda who nursed the two of you back to health!" Sarah said, recalling the big black woman's wise and gentle presence in the little cabin at Harrodstown. "I wonder where Malinda is now? And Mrs. Reynolds and her family? I really enjoyed teaching those little girls!"

"Mrs. Reynolds took her family and Malinda back East soon after you and your Uncle Ethan left the fort to take Dulcie and Sam back to Williamsburg," Ma answered. "We haven't heard from them since then."

"Remember the day I took the Reynolds girls to pick wildflowers and the Indians nearly got us?" Sarah asked.

"Can I ever forget it!" Ma breathed. "Don't you and the baby go out of sight of the cabin, Sarah," she cautioned.

"All right, Ma," Sarah promised, reaching her hands toward Elizabeth and wiggling her fingers invitingly. "Come on, Lizzie," she coaxed.

"Her name's not 'Lizzie,'" Jamie corrected sternly. "It's 'Lizbeth.'"

Sarah glanced quickly at Ma, who responded with a shrug and a grin. "I've been trying not to let her be nicknamed," she explained. "Elizabeth is such a pretty name."

"Sorry!" Sarah said. "Come, Elizabeth, let Sadie dress you and comb your hair, then we'll go pick flowers."

Jamie looked up and smiled at the baby name he had once called Sarah. "Go with Sadie, Lizbeth," he urged. "It'll be fun!"

Hesitantly, Elizabeth raised her little arms. "Go?" she said doubtfully.

Sarah picked her up. "That's right, sweets. We'll go get some pretty flowers for Ma and Jamie."

Elizabeth turned and looked back over Sarah's shoulder as she carried her into the bedroom to change her clothes. She kept peeping around the door frame at Ma while Sarah dressed her, combed her hair, and slipped her tiny deerskin moccasins on her feet. But once she was ready to go, clinging to Sarah's dress with both fists, she let Sarah carry her into the yard.

The morning mist was rapidly burning away. Sarah could see the creek glinting in the sunlight as they made their way into the meadow. The little purple wild asters beckoned all around them.

"Look at all the pretty little flowers, Elizabeth," Sarah said. She plucked a bunch and handed it to her. The baby let go of Sarah with one hand and took the stem. She stuck her little turned-up nose into the blossoms.

"That's right," Sarah encouraged. "Flowers smell good,

don't they, sweets?"

"Good!" Elizabeth agreed, with a shy grin.

"Let's pick a big bouquet for Ma," Sarah said, setting the baby on her feet so she could hold the flowers she picked.

Elizabeth dropped her flower and grasped one growing in front of her. Suddenly it pulled loose from the stem, and Elizabeth, caught off balance, sat down heavily in the tall grass. She looked up at Sarah, her blue eyes wide with surprise, not quite sure whether to laugh or to cry.

Sarah stooped to hug her. "It's all right, sweets," she comforted. "Here, hold these flowers, and I'll get some more."

Quickly, Sarah worked her way across the meadow. Finally, one arm filled with the purple blooms, she turned to pick up Elizabeth with the other. There, almost in front of them, was the big hollow sycamore tree where she had made a playhouse that first year in Kentucky, and where she, Luke, and Jamie had hidden that day three years ago when Ma had nearly been scalped by Indians.

Suddenly, Sarah wondered if her little stick dolls still sat around the rock table she had made, set with the tiny cups and saucers made from acorns.

"Come, Elizabeth," she said, "I want to show you a very special place." She hadn't really wanted to share her secret playhouse with her brothers. Luke teased her too much, and Jamie, back then, had torn things up. But Elizabeth was a little girl. It was likely she would be as happy playing "house" in the hollow tree as Sarah had been.

Sarah set the baby on her feet and led her around the sycamore tree. They went through the opening that led into the small room formed by the hollow walls of the huge tree. She looked around eagerly. There was the rock fireplace she had spent so many hours building. And there were her stick dolls, dressed in scraps of cloth, having their everlasting tea party from acorn cups and saucers and wood chip plates on the rock table.

Elizabeth toddled over to the table. " 'Ittle cup?" she said, reaching for an acorn. Then she noticed the dolls. "Baby!" she cooed.

Suddenly, Sarah gasped. In the middle of the table was a small bouquet of wild asters arranged in a thimble! She had not been here for three years! Who had been playing in her playhouse? Who had placed this fresh bouquet on the dolls' table?

2

Who could have been in her playhouse? Sarah tried to think as she carried Elizabeth and their flowers to the cabin. The baby was too little to come so far from the house by herself.

Could it have been Jamie? He had always been fascinated by the playhouse. With her out of the way in Williamsburg, had her little brother decided to make the playhouse his own? Still, she could not imagine the rambunctious little boy absorbed in anything but his corncob farm, or pretending to fight bears or Indians, or playing with the dog a lady at Harrodstown had given him. She could not imagine him enjoying a dolls' tea party!

Certainly neither Ma nor Pa had been down here playing dolls, and a nearly seventeen-year-old boy like Luke wasn't likely to arrange a bouquet of flowers in Ma's thimble for a dolls' tea party! Luke had never been interested in dolls, but he didn't act like a boy anymore. He didn't even pull her long brown hair or tease her about her green cat's eyes. He had become a man.

If it was none of her family, then who had put the bouquet on the dolls' table?

"Ma, do any of the new families on Stoney Creek have a little girl who might be playing in my old playhouse in the sycamore tree?" Sarah asked, depositing Elizabeth and the flower she was clutching on the braided rug before the hearth. She reached for Ma's teapot to hold her bouquet.

Ma looked up from the wooden mold she was filling with soft, yellow butter. "I can't think of any, Sarah," she said, with a thoughtful frown. "Of course, there's the Larkin girls. But Ruthie is more apt to want to play farm with Jamie than dolls. She's a real little tomboy! And Betsy's got her mind more on a real house with Luke than on a playhouse."

"Well, somebody's been there," Sarah insisted, dipping a gourd full of water from the water bucket to fill the teapot holding her flowers. She set the bouquet in the middle of the wooden table, and stepped back to admire her handiwork.

"Maybe you've just forgotten how you left the playhouse, Sarah," Ma suggested.

Sarah shook her head. "Ma, there's a fresh bouquet of flowers on the dolls' table that must have been put there in the last day or so! And they are in a thimble! I never put a thimble down there."

"A thimble!" Ma repeated. She hurried to her sewing box and rummaged inside it. "Mine is here," she said, holding the thimble up on one finger, "and here's the one your pa put in your stocking that first Christmas in Kentucky." She put the thimbles back in the box and put the top on it. Then she stood staring out the cabin door, as though she could see all the way down over the creek bank and into the hollow tree.

★ Chapter Two ★

"Like I said earlier, Sarah, strange things have been happening around here," she said. "Eggs disappear from their nests. The cow seems to give less milk, as though she has already been partially milked. Just two nights ago, a chicken disappeared from right out of the coop where I had it penned up for fattening."

"Right out of the coop?" Sarah repeated.

Ma nodded. "The strange thing was, there was no sign of the coop being broken into. The door was shut tight with the

wooden latch fastened. It was like someone or something just unfastened it, reached in and took out the chicken, and fastened the door back."

"Could it have been a raccoon, Ma?" Sarah asked. "'Coons will open latches with those little baby hands of theirs."

"Yes, but I never knew a 'coon, or any other animal, to fasten the latch back after it got what it was after!" Ma laughed. Then she shook her head. "It's a real mystery, Sarah! Your pa's even found the millstone swept clean of the leavings from a grinding of corn or wheat. Whoever is raiding our farms is human."

"I forgot that you said the Larkins had lost a cover and somebody else a bearskin, so I guess it's not an animal that's taking things," Sarah agreed. Again, fear traveled down Sarah's spine at the thought, but she had to say it. "Ma, do you think it could be an Indian?"

Ma stopped with the mold of butter poised over a clean cloth. "I don't know, Sarah. Your pa says there's no sign of Indians, and like I said, the dogs don't bark or growl. Whoever comes in the night to raid our place has either got the dogs scared or has made friends with them."

Sarah looked out the cabin window at the dark woods behind them. Anything could be hidden out there in the shadows under those trees, she thought, just waiting for the cover of darkness to creep down to the barn, the mill, the cabin. What if the next time he came, he was not content to raid hens' nests or chicken coops? What if he turned his evil intentions toward the cabin where all of them slept, unaware of danger?

But would a chicken thief decorate a dolls' tea table with flowers? The theft of eggs, milk, and chickens seemed to have no connection with the mystery of who had been playing in the hollow tree. There had to be a young girl around somewhere!

"How many families are living on Stoney Creek now?" Sarah asked.

Ma frowned in concentration. "Well, there's the Larkins, of course, and the Mackeys just beyond them up the creek.

They have five boys, just like stairsteps. The oldest is a little younger than Luke, I reckon, and the youngest was born after they got here, so he's younger than Elizabeth. Then there's an older couple back behind them, the Strausbergs, from Pennsylvania. But they don't have any children."

"No girls except Betsy and Ruthie Larkin?" Sarah asked.

"The Willards, who settled about two miles down the creek from us, have a girl. She's about fifteen or sixteen and eyeing the oldest Mackey boy. I don't doubt he's got his eyes set on her, too. She's a pretty thing, but a little too bold for my liking," Ma added. "I reckon it's a good thing Luke's so set on Betsy Larkin or he might be wandering off down that way."

Sarah had the feeling that, in spite of her laughter, Ma was relieved to have Luke safely out of harm's way. "Are Luke and Betsy planning a wedding soon?" she asked.

"Well, you know the mother of the groom is always the last to know, but I wouldn't be surprised," Ma said. "Luke's been talking about where he might like to build a cabin." She sighed. "He could do a lot worse than to marry Betsy Larkin, though," she said. "She'll make a good wife and a good daughter-in-law, or I miss my guess."

Sarah went over and put her arms around her mother's neck. "I've missed you, Ma," she said, planting a quick kiss on her cheek.

Ma patted Sarah's hand. "I've missed you too, dear, more than you'll ever know!" Then, always one to be embarrassed by any outward show of affection, she gently removed Sarah's arms and picked up the cloth-wrapped cake of butter. She placed it in a small brown crock and held it out to Sarah.

"Run put this in the spring, Sarah, where it will keep cool. And put this pitcher of buttermilk beside it. Your pa and Luke will want some cold buttermilk for supper, and that spring's so cold it will cool down in no time. Oh, and bring me back that small bowl of apples I set on the shelf above the spring. They're the last of the ones I brought from the fort, but they won't keep much longer. I'll make us some fried apples for supper."

"Are things safe down there under the creek bank, out of sight of the cabin, Ma?" Sarah asked in surprise. She knew animals came to drink from the spring too, for she and Luke used to find their footprints in the mud below it.

"I forget, child, how long you've been away!" Ma exclaimed. "Your pa found the source of that spring, a gushing up of clear water out of that outcropping of rock behind the cabin, so cold it hurts my teeth to drink it. He's built us a springhouse over it to protect our things from weather and animals."

Sarah found the springhouse just as Ma had described it, but there was no bowl of apples on the shelf. The springhouse was small, and she searched it thoroughly. The apples just weren't there. She left the springhouse, shut the door and latched it, then hurried back to the cabin.

"I reckon our night visitor has found the springhouse, too," Ma said, when Sarah told her. "Was the door open?"

Sarah shook her head. "No, I had to turn the latch and open it to get to the spring. Whoever or whatever got the apples, and shut the door, just like the chicken coop."

"It's certainly not an animal, then," Ma said. She reached for a basket and handed it to Sarah. "Run gather the eggs, Sarah, before nightfall. Those pesky geese still lay their eggs wherever they please, and you won't be able to find them all, but the hens have mostly taken to laying in the wooden nests your pa built inside the barn."

Sarah went to the barn eagerly. She hadn't been in Pa's new

barn yet, but she had always loved the musky, musty smell of hay mixed with horse sweat and whatever crops Pa had stored there.

Quickly, she gathered the eggs from the hay-filled boxes along one side of the barn, and searched among the haystacks for hidden goose nests.

When Sarah brought back the nearly full basket of eggs and handed it to Ma, she nodded in satisfaction. "We beat him to it this time, I reckon!" Ma said.

Sarah sat down on the sun-warmed doorstep. The sun was sinking behind the trees on the western hills, and already the evening star and a thin sliver of pale new moon hung on the horizon. Off in the woods she heard the inevitable whip-poorwill call, followed by the far-off whooo-whooo of an owl.

Suddenly, Sarah remembered the night she had gone with Pa and Luke to raid a bee tree, and they had found themselves surrounded by the eerie cries of night birds in the dark forest. If Pa hadn't recognized the birdcalls for what they really were, all their scalps might have dangled from Indian belts that night!

Sarah studied the rapidly darkening forest around them. She wondered who was out there, waiting for full dark to cover his evil deeds. But she said nothing as she helped Ma get supper on the table.

Pa and Luke came in, teasing each other about who had cut the most wood that day. Still, Sarah said nothing about her fears, joining the others as they ate hungrily of venison stew from wooden bowls, and cornbread straight from the iron skillet that straddled the fire on legs like a giant spider.

A picture came into her mind of the meals she had shared in the Armstrong house in Williamsburg, with only Meggie outdoing her on sour old Hester Starkey's crisp fried chicken and Aunt Charity's soft white bread, eaten from the dainty white china Ma had given her sister before they left for Kentucky.

Quickly, Sarah pushed the thought away, along with thoughts of how safe she had felt in the snug brick house along well-lit Nicholson Street. There would be no sentry here in the wilderness to call out the hours with a reassuring, "All's well!"

I'm going to keep watch tonight, she promised herself as they all prepared for bed. But it had been a long day, filled with the many emotions of coming home, and almost as soon as her head hit the pillow, she was sound asleep. She didn't even turn over until she heard the faint squawk of a chicken, followed by the restless lowing of a cow.

Sarah sat up carefully so she wouldn't wake Elizabeth or Jamie. She walked barefoot to the window and opened the shutter. The springhouse, under a low-hanging sliver of moon, was a small, hunched shadow under the darker shadows of trees and rocks. She couldn't see the barn on the south side of the cabin, for her window faced west.

She pulled on her stockings and wrapped her cloak about her. Then, carrying her shoes in her hands, she made her way to the cabin's main room where Ma and Pa slept in a bed in the back corner. She could hear Luke snoring upstairs as she slipped out the front door, pulled it to behind her, and sat down on the doorstep to put on her shoes.

The cow mooed softly out in the barn, and she heard the faint snorting and restless stamping of a horse. She eased around the corner of the cabin to where she could just make out the outline of the barn, a somewhat lighter shadow etched across the almost black night sky.

Suddenly, the barn door swung slightly open and a dark figure emerged. She couldn't tell if it was an Indian or not. The door swung shut, and she saw the figure slide the bar across it.

Sarah bit her lip. By the time she could wake Pa and Luke and they could get out here with their guns, the intruder likely would have disappeared into the woods. But what other choice did she have? It was most likely an Indian. If she caught him, he would just overpower her, maybe kill her, and still make his escape.

Sarah eased over to the cabin door, pushed it open, and called softly, "Pa! Someone's in the barn!"

She heard her father's feet hit the floor. He was in the doorway in seconds with his gun in his hands, his nightshirt tucked into his breeches, his shoes on his bare feet.

Sarah looked back at the barn. Nothing moved. Even the cow and horse were still now.

"What's going on, Sary?" Pa whispered loudly. "What did you see?"

"Someone came out of the barn and shut the door, Pa," she whispered back. "I don't see him now. I think he's gone."

"Wait here!" Pa ordered, striding off across the yard and into the barn lot.

"Pa, be careful!" she called.

Pa disappeared behind the barn. "Halt, you rascal!" she heard him yell. Then the gun went off. Sarah ran to the fence, straining her eyes to see in the darkness.

"What's going on?" Luke asked sleepily from the doorway.

"Someone was in the barn," she answered. "Pa just shot at him, or he just shot at Pa!"

Luke went back into the cabin and soon came out, wearing his nightshirt and his shoes. Like Pa, he carried a gun, and like Pa, he went straight to the barn and disappeared around it.

In a few minutes, Sarah saw two shadows come around the other side of the barn and go inside. Then they came out, shut and barred the door, and came toward the cabin.

"I think I hit him. I saw him stumble when I shot, but he ran on into the woods," Pa said, as he and Luke came into the yard. "And he got another chicken, the rascal!"

"Do you think it was an Indian, Pa?" Luke asked. "Should we try to pick up his tracks? If you winged him, he may leave a trail of blood."

"If it is an Indian, he can see far better than we can in that black forest, son, and there's no way we could pick up his trail tonight," Pa answered. "No, whoever he is, he's in no danger of being caught this time."

"But, Pa, we can't just let him go on taking our chickens!" Luke protested. "Ma says the foxes and 'possums have already thinned out the flock until there's barely enough to lay the eggs we need, and hardly any fryers left."

"That's what he got tonight, too," Pa said. "That frying rooster your ma was fattening for a Sunday's dinner."

Like little Megan back in Williamsburg, fried chicken was Sarah's "fav'rite," but she guessed they wouldn't be having any soon. "I hope he enjoys it!" she muttered spitefully.

Back in her room, she eased into bed beside the still sleeping Elizabeth. She lay there listening to Pa's voice in the next room, explaining to Ma what had happened.

The cabin grew still and heavy with sleep, but Sarah couldn't seem to doze off again. For a long time, she lay in the big bed, staring at the shutter that covered the window, wondering if their visitor would be back tonight. She supposed, though, that he had taken what he wanted this time and wouldn't return until he was hungry again.

Sarah remembered how Ma had fed the Little Captain when the Indian had come into their camp seeking food when they were first making their way to Kentucky. If the hungry thief would just ask, Ma would be sure to feed him!

Finally, Sarah sank into a troubled sleep, dreaming of an Indian with chicken feathers in his long black braids, chasing her around the barn.

When she awoke, the pale light of dawn outlined the shutter and she could hear a rooster crowing out by the barn. At least their visitor hadn't taken their last rooster. Yet.

The nights grew lighter, bathed by the glow of a harvest moon and many stars that made it almost as bright as day outside. Sarah supposed that was why their visitor did not come sneaking around for the next few nights. Pa and Luke had not been able to find a trail of blood, so they guessed Pa's shot had scared off their intruder, rather than injuring him. Ma still suspected that some of the goose eggs were missing, but the cow gave her full measure of milk and the chicken coop went undisturbed.

The days passed busily as Sarah helped her family prepare for winter. She had forgotten how much work must be done in a place where everything they had depended on their storing it somehow before the cold descended upon them. In Williamsburg, they had worked to store things too, and little was wasted. But there was always John Green-how's store and the other shops on Duke of Gloucester Street where they could buy the things they needed.

The good harvest weather held though, and soon they had a barn full of hay, a good stock of wheat and corn in Pa's new mill, and the walls of the cabin were covered with strings of drying beans, peppers, and herbs that gave the place a pleasant, spicy smell.

"The first cold snap in November, we'll have to do a hog and a beef killing, and maybe get us a deer to salt down," Pa said, as they stored the last of the garden's sweet potatoes and cabbages in a deep hole to keep them from freezing.

"We need a real smokehouse, Hiram," Ma suggested. "That little shed out back won't hold as many hams, bacons, and shoulders as I'd like to have curing in the smoke of a hickory fire, and we need a bigger salt box."

Sarah's mouth watered. There wasn't much she liked better than a big slice of cured ham or a few cakes of spicy sausage with her eggs! But she hated the messy job of processing meat.

"I've got a big poplar log laid by to hollow out this winter. By this time next year, we'll have a salt box to end all salt boxes!" Pa promised. "Until then, though, I'm afraid we'll just have to move the meat in and out in shifts, and hope it absorbs enough salt to keep."

"I hope we've got enough salt to last us," Ma said. "I didn't like being here alone with the children while you went to the salt springs with the men from the fort."

"I know, Della," Pa said. "I was worried the whole time I was gone that Indians would attack our place, with no one but Luke here to protect you. But the good Lord took care of us, just like He always does."

"I can't imagine why we haven't had a major attack by Indians during this pretty weather," Luke said, as he forked hay over the vegetables they had placed in the hole. "They don't call this time of year 'Indian Summer' for nothing!"

"They probably just hit some other settlements this time, but it is their last chance before winter sets in," Pa agreed, placing half-logs across the top of the hole. "They'll be too busy keeping warm and keeping food in their children's stomachs to bother with us settlers much this winter, I reckon. It's going to be a cold one!"

"How do you know it's going to be a cold winter, Pa?" Sarah asked. She knew Pa could predict the weather from the sunrise or the sunset, or from the way the moon hung in the sky, but how could he know what the weather was going to be months from now?

Pa pointed to one of the logs, where a fat, furry caterpillar was seeking a place to hide from the cold. "Look at the size of the band around the middle of that wooly bear," he said. "A wide band of red-brown around him with hardly any black at each end would mean a short time of bad weather at each end of winter, with a long spell of good weather in the middle. But there's hardly any red-brown on him at all. That's a sure sign of a long, hard winter."

"You believe the color of a caterpillar can tell you all that, Pa?" Sarah asked in amazement.

"Well, there's other signs," Pa insisted. "The bark on the trees is thick, and there's plenty of acorns, hickory nuts, and walnuts this year, another sure sign that the good Lord is providing extra food for His squirrels, chipmunks, and other critters in a hard winter to come."

"There's an abundance of berries and seeds for the birds, too, but I always like to save bread crumbs for them to eat when other things are covered with snow," Ma said. "There's just nothing prettier than a snow-covered cedar tree filled with bright red cardinals!" she added.

"I think I like the little gray and white titmouse best," Sarah put in, "with those little touches of blue and orange and that pretty little topknot on his head."

"I know he's a rascal among birds," Pa broke in, "but

there's not much prettier than a thieving old blue jay when he spreads those blue and white wings and sails off through the air."

"Speaking of thieves, I just hope ours doesn't find this storage hole," Ma said. "The few things I've missed from the garden, we can live without, but I'd sure hate to lose all our winter vegetables after we've harvested and stored them, or our meat after we've gone to all the trouble to cure it!"

"I think that most likely, it was an Indian, and he's headed on up north toward their villages for the winter," Pa said.

"He might think he's got it too good around here to leave," Ma said doubtfully. "Maybe he's found himself a cozy den up there in the woods somewhere, and he's all holed up for the winter with his woven cover and his bear skin to keep him warm, and with our provisions to keep him well fed!"

Pa flung the last half-log over the hole and brushed his hands. "Well, I promise you one thing, ladies and gentlemen, that thieving rascal has about stolen his last from the Hiram Moore family! I don't think he'll risk coming out in the light of that big harvest moon we've had these past few nights, but the next dark night, I aim to sleep with my clothes on and my gun handy. We'll see how far he gets with my Sunday dinner!"

Sarah laughed with the rest of them, but she had a feeling that the twinkle in Pa's Irish blue eyes didn't mean he wasn't serious about what he said.

4

The very next night, with clouds covering the moon and a brewing storm darkening the sky, Sarah awoke to the loud squawking of a chicken and Hunter's frenzied barking out in the barn.

Sarah eased out of bed without waking Elizabeth, but Jamie turned over in his trundle bed beside her and murmured drowsily, "Whatsa matter?"

"Nothing, sweets. Go back to sleep," Sarah urged softly. Surprisingly, he obeyed.

Sarah ran into the next room and found Ma standing by the door in her long nightgown with a thick braid of curly brown hair hanging down her back.

Pa was over by the fireplace, fully dressed, transferring bullets from the tin box on the mantel to his deerskin pouch. He slung its strap over one shoulder and grabbed the gun he had leaned against the fireplace. He was out the door and halfway across the yard when Luke came stumbling down the stairs, wearing breeches and his nightshirt. He was barefoot, but he carried a gun. He raced out the door after Pa.

Sarah followed them as far as the yard fence. She could hear

Hunter still barking furiously and the horses thrashing around in their stalls. The cow gave a low "mooooo" followed by her calf's soft "maaaaa."

Suddenly, a figure came out of the barn and reached up overhead to fasten the door. Something was wrong with that picture, but Sarah couldn't figure out what it was.

"Stop, or I'll shoot!" Pa yelled. Sarah heard him cock his gun.

The figure looked over its shoulder, dropped the bar, and ran around the corner of the barn.

Luke ran around the barn to the right, and Pa to the left. A gunshot exploded.

"Did you get him, Pa?" Luke called.

"Naw, he got clean away!" Pa called back.

★ Chapter Four ★

Soon, Sarah saw them coming back across the barn lot.

"It appeared to me our thief was a mite small," she heard Pa say as they came into the yard.

"You're right, Pa!" Luke exclaimed. "I hadn't thought about it, but his head didn't even reach the bar on the barn door!"

Suddenly, Sarah knew what was wrong with the picture of the thief reaching up to bar the barn door. The other night, he had been tall enough to reach the bar without stretching. Tonight, it was all he could do to reach it! How could that be explained? Were there two thieves?

Sarah spent a restless night, watching the window, listening for strange sounds, wondering about the shadowy threat that now hovered over their home. From the first day they had settled on Stoney Creek, they had faced dangers from Indians, wild animals, storms, and illness. But they never had faced danger from criminals who came to rob or to harm them.

Sarah mentioned this to Ma the next morning, but Ma shook her head at her warningly, glancing at Jamie who was playing with his farm in the corner of the room. Sarah knew Ma didn't want to frighten the little boy. She would just have to wait until she and Ma were alone to discuss it.

Soon after the noon meal, there was a knock at the door and a voice called, "It's Rowena, Della!"

Jamie ran to the door and threw it open with a happy shout of "Ruthie!"

Mrs. Larkin and Ruthie came into the cabin, and the two children immediately began some game with Jamie's corncob farm.

Then Sarah caught her breath. Behind them was Betsy! Sarah started toward her, then stopped, suddenly shy at seeing her friend after being so far away from her for so many months.

Then Betsy smiled, the same friendly smile she had given Sarah the first day the Larkins had come to Stoney Creek. It started with her generous mouth and spread to her clear blue eyes. Instantly, the months and miles fell away, and Sarah ran to give her a hug.

"Sarah, I just can't believe what a young lady you have grown to be!" Mrs. Larkin said. "And how pretty you are! If that oldest Mackey boy ever sets eyes on you, he'll be over here like a bee after honey!"

Sarah felt a blush creep over her face. She knew she wasn't all that pretty, but she supposed it was nice of Mrs. Larkin to say so, even if it did embarrass her, especially in front of Betsy.

Ma laughed. "Trace Mackey has got his eyes set on the Willard girl. Now, there's a bold one for you!"

"You've got that right!" Mrs. Larkin agreed. "She's a pretty little thing, with those green eyes and that thick curly hair, but she flirts with everything in breeches! I've even seen her making eyes at Luke in church, and he and Betsy practically ready to call in the preacher!"

"Oh, Ma!" Betsy protested, and it was her turn to blush.

"Speaking of preachers," Mrs. Larkin went on, "did you hear that we're going to have a real preaching service at the church? Some preacher is riding through the settlements holding services, and a week from Sunday it's our turn."

Ma shook her head. "I hadn't heard, but it will be good to have a service, something more than our men reading the Scriptures and leading a few hymns."

"It's so good to see you, Sarah!" Betsy said, drawing her away from their mothers toward the other room. "Come, tell me all about Williamsburg! It must be an exciting place, with the capital there, and all! Are the homes very grand? I suppose they would laugh at us here in the backwoods in our rough log cabins."

"You just wouldn't believe how gorgeous some of the homes are in Williamsburg!" Sarah answered. "Some of them are nothing short of mansions. And there's the Governor's Palace with its beautiful gardens and graceful white swans swimming on the canal. I wish you could see it, Betsy!"

"So do I Sarah, but you know, I'm happy here on Stoney Creek. I'll be perfectly content with a log cabin like this, if Luke ever gets around to asking Pa for me. Sometimes I wonder. . . ."

As they chatted, Sarah felt a growing sadness. She and Betsy lived within walking distance of each other, yet it was easy to see that their worlds were far apart. Betsy's thoughts and dreams were of marriage and keeping house and raising children, but *I'm not ready for any of that!* Sarah thought with a shudder.

Sarah admired Ma greatly. She worked so hard to provide a good home for her family, even here in the wilderness. *Especially* here in the wilderness! Sarah corrected herself. Ma always had worked hard back in Miller's Forks, Virginia, but she had had some time for fun, for picnics and games and singing. Now, she just seemed tired and determined to get done what she had to do.

Sarah didn't mind helping Ma with the house and meals, or with caring for little Jamie and Elizabeth, but even though she had little interest in dolls now, she still would rather go down to her playhouse in the hollow tree and dress those stick dolls than to be responsible for children of her own. And she'd rather settle in for a rainy afternoon with a good book than cope with the responsibilities of a home.

"What do you want to do, Sarah?" Betsy asked then, as

though she could read her thoughts. "Here, I've been rattling on and on about my life, and you've hardly said a word."

"Oh, I don't know, Betsy. I think I might like to try teaching school for a while. But there isn't any schoolhouse here."

"Sarah, there's the church building the men put up as soon as we all had roofs over our heads. It's empty all week. Why couldn't you start a school there? It's just one room, but it already has benches in it, and there's a fireplace. Luke could make you some wooden paddles to write on, and sticks burnt in the fireplace make good charcoal pencils."

Sarah's heart beat faster. Was it possible? She hadn't really thought to begin her career as a teacher until she was older, at least sixteen. But she was fourteen, and the children she would be teaching were much younger. She handled a five year old and a two year old every day. Surely she could handle a few more!

"I don't know, Betsy," she said, "but I would like to try. Do you really think they would let me?"

"I would think the families around here would be grateful to have some education for their children," Betsy assured her.

"Something's got to be done about this thief!" Rowena Larkin said loudly in the next room. Sarah could imagine that Ma was shaking her head warningly at her, but Mrs. Larkin went right on with her comments. "Why, the Mackey's youngest boy's best homespun breeches and good blue shirt were taken right off the clothes pole behind their cabin the other day, in broad daylight!"

"You don't say!" Sarah heard Ma answer.

She and Betsy exchanged glances, and went back to the other room to listen.

"Now, what on Earth would the thief want with a child's

clothes?" Mrs. Larkin was saying. "He's a grown man, for he's been spotted a time or two."

"I think there's two of them," Sarah said, and she explained about the different heights of the two figures she had seen at the barn.

"Well, I never!" Mrs. Larkin breathed. "Then that's why the child's clothes were taken. One of them is either a child or a very small man.

"I've heard that some criminals are coming to Kentucky, either to hide from the penalties for their crimes back East, or to start over. I wouldn't think there would be much here in the backwoods to tempt them otherwise," Sarah said.

"Still, it appears that there are at least two of them right here on Stoney Creek!" Mrs. Larkin said. "And they steal from some of us nearly every night."

"Yes, but they seem to take only food and covering," Ma said doubtfully.

Mrs. Larkin laughed. "There's none of us got anything else they could steal!"

"I reckon you're right," Ma agreed, joining her laughter.

"I say the men ought to call a meeting after church tomorrow and figure out what to do about it," Mrs. Larkin said firmly.

Soon after that, she and her girls left, and Sarah went to help Ma prepare supper.

"I don't like losing things to a thief," Ma said, as she cut up a squirrel Pa had shot that morning and rolled it in flour for frying. "But I can't begrudge food to the hungry or covers to keep some homeless person warm."

Sarah smiled as she sliced potatoes into a skillet. "I know you can't, Ma. Remember how you fed the Little Captain that night on the trail as we traveled to Kentucky? I've never known you to turn away anything cold or hungry."

"Still, we can't go on losing our hard-earned belongings this way. I reckon Rowena is right. The men need to do something," Ma mused. "But if one of them is a child . . ."

"Maybe one of the families here would give it a home," Sarah suggested. "What about those something-burgs you said lived behind the Mackeys? Didn't you say they have no children?"

"The Strausbergs. No, there's just the two of them. But they are older people, Sarah. I don't know that they should be taking in a child to raise, especially one who already has made his way as a thief! Anyway, we don't know that one of them is a child. He may just be small of stature."

Sarah supposed Ma was right. At any rate, there was nothing any of them could do about it until the thieves were caught.

5

Sarah knew Ma would be yelling for her if she didn't get back to the house with the cream for their morning coffee, but she couldn't help dawdling a little as she followed the path to the springhouse. It was such a beautiful morning, with the sunlight bathing the hills and the meadows in a golden glow. Every breath of air was filled with the mellow scent of dying leaves, mingled with a hint of smoke from Ma's breakfast fire, rising straight and true from one of Pa's carefully made rock chimneys.

It was impossible to reach the springhouse door without stepping on the leaves of the spearmint plants that grew thickly underfoot on both sides of the clear, cold stream, and Sarah breathed deeply of the pungent odor. She reached down to pluck a leaf to chew, savoring the cool, minty freshness in her mouth.

Sarah unlatched the springhouse door, bent to enter through the low doorway, then waited a moment for her eyes to adjust to the dimness inside. She stooped down to retrieve the small crock of cream from the spring, then as she straightened, her gaze fell on the shelf above the spring where the bowl of apples once had set, before the thief helped himself to it.

Sarah gasped. The bowl was back! She knew it had not been there when Ma sent her to look for it the other day, nor had it been there yesterday evening when she came for a fresh bucket of water. But it was there now, and there was something in it.

Carefully, Sarah eased the bowl from the shelf and discovered that it was full of persimmons!

"What kind of thief would try to pay for what he stole?" Ma said when she showed her the bowl and its offering of small orange fruit. "But that's obviously what he's trying to do!"

"Then he owes us for two frying chickens, several dozen eggs, and who knows how many quarts of milk!" Pa said, coming in the doorway with Luke behind him.

"But, Hiram, this puts the whole thing in a new light," Ma said. "Our visitor is not a real thief. He's just hungry, and he has a conscience. He feels bad about having to steal to live, and he wants to make amends."

"Pshaw!" Pa muttered.

"Then how do you explain these persimmons?" Ma insisted. When Pa didn't answer, she went on, "that tells me we have nothing to fear from our thief."

"Except the loss of half our livestock and provisions," Pa retorted, sitting down and pulling his chair up under the table. "Are we having breakfast this morning, madam?" he asked, deliberately changing the subject.

Ma handed Sarah a wooden bowl to hold the biscuits and went to dish up the fried squirrel and gravy, but all through breakfast she wore a satisfied expression that said, "I won that argument, even though he won't admit it!"

After breakfast, Sarah peeled potatoes to go into the kettle of cabbage seasoned with ham that Ma had bubbling over the fire. Then she spent the rest of the morning straightening the cabin and keeping Jamie and Elizabeth out of the way while Ma made persimmon preserves from most of the fruits their visitor had left.

Pa and Luke had taken lunch with them to the forest where they were cutting more firewood, so Sarah, Ma, Jamie, and Elizabeth made a quick meal of cabbage, potatoes, and cornbread. When the dishes were washed and the kitchen in order, Ma got out her mixing bowl and a long-handled wooden spoon.

"Do you mind if I take Elizabeth down to our playhouse, Ma?" Sarah asked. "That is, if you don't need me for a little while."

"That will be all right, Sarah, but be careful," Ma cautioned. "Our visitor apparently was around last night. He could be anywhere today."

"Can I go with you to the creek, Sarah?" Jamie asked. "I promise I won't go near the playhouse."

Sarah felt a twinge of guilt for all the times she had scolded him for tearing up her dolls and knocking over her rock furniture. "Of course, you can go, Jamie. You can go with us to the playhouse, if you like."

"No, thank you," he said seriously. "I need to get some rocks to build a dam across this creek here so my horses and cows will have a watering hole."

Sarah shared an amused grin with Ma as they watched the little boy place his pinecone animals around his imaginary creek.

"We won't be gone long, Ma," she promised then, picking up Elizabeth and holding out her free hand to Jamie. Elizabeth laughed and clutched at Sarah's dress for safety, but Jamie scampered out the door and into the yard.

"Take your time," Ma answered. "I'm going to make us a cake for supper with the rest of these persimmons."

"I didn't know you could make a cake out of persimmons," Sarah said in surprise. She had eaten many a persimmon after frost had cut it loose from its tree and let it drop to the ground. She had even eaten a green one once and deeply regretted it. Her mouth had stayed puckered up like a drawstring purse for hours afterward!

"Well, I've never made one," Ma admitted, "but I'd never made preserves out of them until this morning, either. We always had plenty of other fruits and berries back in Miller's Forks. Here, I try not to waste anything, even persimmons!"

"I just hope they all are ripe!" Sarah chuckled as she left the cabin with Elizabeth in her arms. "Wait for us, Jamie!" she called, not wanting him to venture too close to the deep pools that lay below the creek bank.

"Don't go too far!" Ma called from inside the cabin. "Remember our visitor!"

And snakes, and Indians, and wild animals from the forest, Sarah added under her breath. Kentucky had always been full of dangers. And now they had this extra concern of a mysterious stranger creeping around their homesteads in the shadows, stealing their food.

How did their nighttime visitor come and go? He had run into the woods behind the barn the other night, but that didn't mean he couldn't be lurking on this side of the cabin today. The mill was just below the playhouse, and Pa said if he didn't clean the millstone immediately when he finished a big runoff of corn or wheat, the leftover meal and flour disappeared overnight.

Elizabeth reached for a wild aster, and Sarah stooped to let her pick one. "Pity?" she said, holding it up for Sarah to see.

"Yes, sweets, the flower is pretty," Sarah agreed, hurrying on to where Jamie had stopped dead still on the top of the bank.

"Pity?" Elizabeth said again, holding the flower out to Jamie.

"Shhhh, Lizbeth!" Jamie whispered, as they stopped beside him. "I hear somebody humming."

Elizabeth looked at Sarah with wide, hurt eyes. Sarah patted her on the back, as she listened for humming. "I don't hear anything, Jamie," she whispered. "Are you sure you didn't just hear the creek murmuring over the rocks?"

He shook his head. "No, Sarah, somebody was humming, down there inside the hollow tree!"

Suddenly, there was a flash of blue as someone ran out of the tree's opening and around to its other side.

"There!" Jamie yelled triumphantly. "I told you somebody was in there!"

For a moment, Sarah stood frozen to her spot on the creek bank. Then she hurried down to the creek and over to the tree, but whoever had been hiding behind it was gone.

The sound of a rock turning drew her attention to the other side of the creek just in time to glimpse gray homespun breeches and a blue shirt disappearing into the trees.

Should I follow him? Sarah wondered. But with Elizabeth and Jamie to see to, it was unlikely that she could catch him, even if she hadn't been afraid to try.

Deciding the playhouse would now be safe, Sarah carried Elizabeth to the hollow tree and set her on her feet. She toddled over to the rock table. "Baby!" she crowed, reaching for a stick doll.

Sarah's eyes widened. The doll's rag dress had been replaced with a red oak leaf. She looked at the other dolls. All of them wore new red, orange, or yellow dresses made of autumn leaves! In the fireplace was a pretend fire of red and orange leaves, and the wood chip plates held a doll's meal of red buckberries and orange persimmons!

Was it the thief, after all, who played here in the hollow tree? But why would he want to dress and feed stick dolls? Was he insane? Had he escaped from some asylum back East and come here to hide in the woods and . . . and what? Were they in real danger from him? Would he come creeping out of the woods some dark night to murder them in their beds?

"We must tell your father about this as soon as he comes in," Ma said when Sarah told her about the visitor to the playhouse.

"He was humming!" Jamie put in excitedly, "kind of humming like you do when you try to get Lizbeth to sleep, Ma."

"I didn't hear anything," Sarah admitted, "but I did see somebody run from the tree and into the woods across the creek."

"Baby pity!" Elizabeth said to Ma, holding out the stick doll dressed in its red oak leaf. Sarah had forgotten she had it.

"See, Ma," she said. "I left those dolls dressed in scraps of cloth. Now they're all wearing leaves, just like Adam and Eve!"

Ma shook her head. "I just don't know what to make of it—a thief who risks capture to try to pay for his thieving and to play in a little girl's playhouse with stick dolls!"

"I've never heard anything like it!" Pa said when they told him the story over supper. "A thief playing with dolls!"

★ Chapter Five ★

"He's got to be as crazy as a cow eating hemp weed!" Luke exclaimed, daubing butter on another potato and spearing a chunk of it with his fork. "By the way, I'm going over to the Larkins for a while this evening," he added.

Pa's hand stopped in midair holding a piece of cornbread dipped in cabbage juice. "What a surprise!" he teased before popping the bread in his mouth.

"You spend more time at the Larkins than you do at home, son!" Ma said. "Maybe Rowena and Mark will just adopt you."

"I don't think that's what Luke has in mind!" Pa teased, and they all laughed as Luke, red-faced, left the cabin on his way to see Betsy.

Thinking of Betsy reminded Sarah of their conversation about starting a school. "The church building must stand empty all week," she began, as she helped Ma clear away the supper things. "Do you think it could be used for a school?"

"Why, that's a good idea, Sarah!" Ma said. "There are several little boys here on Stoney Creek who could use some schooling, Jamie among them. Would you be willing to teach them?"

"Oh, yes! That is, if you and Pa think I could," she answered, suddenly unsure of herself.

"You had great success teaching the Reynolds' children at Harrodstown last year," Ma assured her. "Their ma was very pleased. And you have a way with Jamie and Elizabeth. I think you'd make a good teacher, dear."

Sarah felt her face flush at Ma's rare praise.

"Why not?" Pa said. "I'll bring it up at church Sunday, Sary, and we'll see what the people of Stoney Creek have to say about schooling for their children."

"I'm sure Luke will carve me some wooden paddles to mark with the alphabet and numerals so I can teach reading, writing, and figuring," Sarah said excitedly. "That and the Bible was all the teacher at Fort Harrod had. If I can use your Bible . . ."

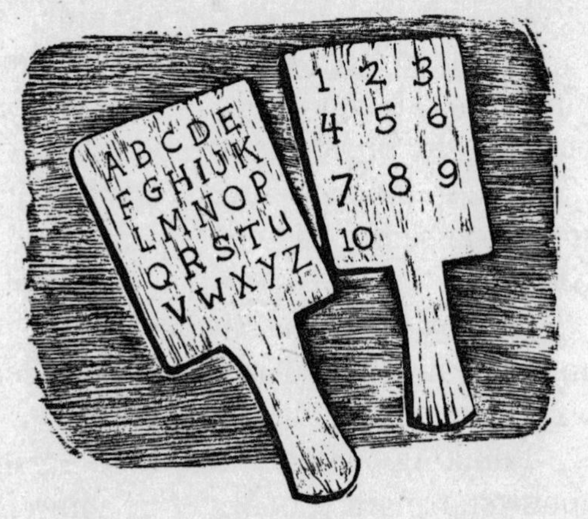

"Whoa there, Sary girl!" Pa cautioned. "Don't get your hopes set on it yet. There's no guarantee that our neighbors want a school here on Stoney Creek at this time, and none that they want their church building used for such a purpose. All we can do is ask, and I promise you I will, next Sunday."

Sarah knew the subject was closed for now, so she said no more about it as she put Elizabeth to bed, then prepared for bed herself. "Please, God," she prayed silently, "if it is Your will, work it all out for me! I want to do more than help tend babies and scrub floors. I'll still do all those things to help Ma, if I can just have something else besides that to fill my days here in the wilderness."

Outside her bedroom window, the bright harvest moon lit the meadow like a thousand candles. Suddenly, Sarah remembered the thief. But surely no thief in his right mind would venture out on such a night! Sarah crawled under the cozy covers beside Elizabeth. Of course, no one claimed their thief was in his right mind, but he must know they had seen him run from the hollow tree. He likely was miles from Stoney Creek by now.

Sunday morning dawned crisp and cold, and Sarah was grateful for the warmth of her heavy cloak over her blue silk dress. She and her family walked up the creek bank to the little cabin just beyond the Larkins' place that the men of Stoney Creek had built for their worship services.

Ma had wrapped her shawl around her shoulders and around Elizabeth in her arms. Jamie had on a heavy buckskin shirt just like Pa's and Luke's, and he had picked up a stick along the way to carry like the guns his pa and brother carried.

"Why are you taking your guns to church?" Sarah couldn't help asking. She had never seen guns in church, but then she had never attended church in the wilderness before.

"Sary, in the wilderness a man needs to carry his gun wherever he goes," Pa answered. "You just never know what you'll run into on the trail, and it's always better to be safe than sorry."

That made sense, Sarah thought, as she inspected the log

cabin before them, then followed her family inside.

The building was small, but snug. Sarah took a seat on a rough, backless bench beside Ma and Elizabeth, about halfway between the door and the pulpit up front. Jamie looked at Pa and Luke, sitting across the center aisle on a similar bench, then took a seat beside Sarah.

Sarah saw Luke craning his neck to watch for Betsy coming in the back door, and Sarah gave him a knowing smirk when she caught his eye. He glowered at her.

A man Sarah didn't know walked down front and faced them. He called out the first line to "Amazing Grace," and they all sang it. Then he called out the second line, and they followed his lead again and again until the song was done and he started a new one.

After they had sung three hymns this way, Pa got up and read from the Scriptures, his favorite verses: John 3:16 and Proverbs 3:5, 6. Then Mark Larkin led in prayer.

"Ladies and gentlemen, that concludes our service for today," Mr. Larkin said, after he had finished praying, "but we have a serious matter to discuss. I don't think there's one among us who has not suffered at the hands of this thief who has made his way to Stoney Creek. The question is, what are we going to do about it?"

"All I know is I can't afford to lose another cover!" Mrs. Larkin said.

"And my boy, Samuel, sure does need his extra pants and shirt!" a woman Sarah took to be Mrs. Mackey said, making everybody laugh.

"I say we should hunt him down like the criminal he is and shoot him!" shouted another man Sarah did not know.

"Now, Willard, that may be a bit drastic," Pa said. "We think there are two thieves, and one of them is either a child or he is very small." Pa went on to explain about the figures they had seen leaving their barn. There was a buzz of conversation around the room, and many puzzled faces.

"You know, come to think of it, there's more strange goings on than we may have realized," Mrs. Mackey said. "Our thief tried to pay for Sammy's shirt and pants with a basket of hickory nuts. Of course, Sammy can't wear hickory nut shells!" They all laughed again.

Ma related the story of the persimmons they had found in place of their missing apples. "It seems that at least one of our thieves has a conscience," she said.

"Nonsense!" a woman called out. "My Will is right. These thieves should be hunted down and shot. Who knows what terrible crimes they've committed back East. They might murder us all in our beds some dark night!"

"Let's form a hunting party this afternoon and go after them!" the man called Will suggested.

"But what if one of them is a child?" Ma asked indignantly. "Will you shoot him, too?"

"I think we should wait and watch until he, or they, visit us again. If we are ready, we can capture them," Pa suggested. "Once we know more about the persons we are dealing with, we can make decisions about what to do with them."

"That's a goot plan," a man with a heavy German accent agreed. *That must be Mr. Strausberg,* Sarah thought, *and that must be his wife, the mousy-looking little woman in black sitting across from him.*

"How many vote to wait and watch," Mark Larkin asked. There was a chorus of "yeas" and two surly "nays," from Will and his wife. Their pretty, auburn-haired daughter was looking over the room, flashing her green eyes first at Luke, then at the Mackey boy, and even at Mark Larkin as he stood up front conducting the meeting!

Ma was right, Sarah thought. *She is a bold one.*

"That settles it then," Mr. Larkin concluded. "We'll wait and watch."

As the meeting began to break up, Mr. Larkin called for their attention again. "Don't forget that we will have a visiting preacher next Sunday!" he reminded them. "And we either need to plan a dinner on the grounds, or we need one of you to volunteer to feed and maybe house him."

Sarah saw Mr. Strausberg's hand go up. "Ve haf plenty of room in our house and at our table," he said. Mrs. Stausberg nodded, the black rose on her black straw bonnet nodding in agreement.

Pa stood up. "There's one more matter I'd like to bring up," he said, and Sarah held her breath as he suggested using the church building for a school.

"Did you say your Sarah is willing to teach this school?" the man who had led the singing asked.

"Yes, Mackey, she is, if you all are willing to have her," Pa answered.

"She appears a mite young to teach. Has she got the training?" Mrs. Willard asked.

"She's got more education than all the rest of us put together!" Mrs. Larkin assured her. "How long did you study in Williamsburg, Sarah?" she asked.

"She studied there with tutors for two years," Ma answered. "One of them called Sarah her star pupil!" she added proudly.

Sarah saw a skeptical smirk touch Mrs. Willard's lips.

"It sounds good to me," Mrs. Mackey said. "My little ruffians could use some polishing!"

"The church building belongs to all of us here on Stoney

Creek," Pa said. "How do those of you who have no children to send to the school feel about using the building for a school during the week?"

"Mama?" Mr. Strausberg asked, leaning across the aisle to study his wife's face. At her nod, he said, "Mama and me haf no one to send to the school, but ve belief the little kinder should be taught their letters and their numbers. Ve haf no problem vit using the church house for such a purpose."

Pa looked directly at the Willards then, the only ones who had voiced questions. "And how do you folks feel about it?" he asked.

Sarah saw Mrs. Willard look at her two red-headed boys, who were into a silent scuffle over something. She sighed, then gave her husband a pleading look. Sarah wondered if she were thinking of the freedom she would have each day while the boys were in school.

"I reckon we could give it a try, but we'll be keeping a sharp eye on this school," Mr. Willard warned.

"That's settled then," Mr. Larkin said. "We'll give Sarah a day to get ready. Folks, our first fall term of school on Stoney Creek will begin this coming Tuesday, and go until . . . Christmas?" He looked questioningly at Sarah, then at Pa.

Pa looked at Sarah, then nodded. "Unless the weather gets bad before then," he said.

Then the meeting was over, and they were outside. Sarah felt a thrill of excitement run through her. She was going to be a school teacher, and she wasn't even fifteen yet! She looked around for someone to share her excitement.

The men had gathered in a group to discuss plans to catch the thieves. The women had formed another clump to carry on conversations about their ailments and their children.

Obviously not a part of either group, Sarah looked around for Betsy and saw her off by the corner of the church talking earnestly with Luke. The bold Miss Willard was flirting openly with the oldest Mackey boy.

Sarah turned and walked over to where the younger children had begun a game of “Run, Sheep, Run” in the meadow. There just wasn’t anybody else here for her, she thought, joining in the game to Jamie’s and Ruthie’s delight.

Maybe she would enjoy teaching school, she thought as she was tagged to become the wolf and began to chase one of the little red-haired Willard boys. She liked children. They were usually eager to learn, and they were interesting. At least their conversation did not center around who they were going to marry or how many of their young ones had just had the measles!

As her family made their way home, Sarah’s thoughts were taken up with plans for her new school. If only she could have some of the books their first tutor in Williamsburg had shared with her and her cousins—books about magical, faraway places like London and Paris and Rome, books that carried the reader far away from the everyday sameness of home!

Sarah’s Uncle Ethan had promised to send her some books. If she wrote and asked him, she was sure he would send some as soon as he could. Meanwhile, unless some of the other families had books she could borrow, she would just have to make do with Pa’s big black Bible and the copy of *Pilgrim’s Progress* her uncle had given her.

“Something’s wrong,” Pa said, interrupting her thoughts. Sarah was surprised to see that they were home and had stopped just outside the yard fence.

“What is it, Hiram?” Ma whispered.

He shook his head uncertainly. “I don’t know. I’ve just got

that prickly feeling up and down my spine and that sinking sensation in my bones that tells me something's not right," Pa whispered back. "I think somebody's been here while we were away."

Sarah felt a shiver travel down her own spine, as Pa cocked his gun. She was glad he had carried it with him this morning.

"Della, you and the young ones take shelter there behind the woodpile," Pa ordered. "I wish Luke had come on home with us instead of gallivanting off to the Larkins for Sunday dinner!" Sarah heard him mutter as he walked quietly toward the cabin.

She peered over the stacked wood, as Pa slowly pushed open the cabin door and disappeared inside. "May the good Lord have mercy upon us!" Sarah heard him exclaim. Then he called, "Della, come here, quick!"

Ma looked at Sarah with wide, frightened eyes. She thrust Elizabeth into Sarah's arms, and pushed Jamie over close to her. Then she ran across the yard and disappeared into the cabin.

Sarah hesitated, then hearing no sign of battle, followed her parents into the cabin. She threw a quick glance around the room. Everything seemed to be in place. There were no hatchet marks on the table or burning embers smoldering on the floor as there had been the day the Indians came that first year in Kentucky. There didn't even seem to be anything missing. Ma's wooden dishes and chipped, flowered teapot sat in the corner cupboard, the mug of spoons and forks beside them.

"What's going on?" Sarah asked. "Everything seems . . ." Then her gaze fell on something in Pa's hand, something that reflected the faint light of the smoldering fire in rainbow colors.

"Pa, where did you get that brooch?" she gasped.

"It was here on the table," he answered. "I saw it the minute I came through the door."

"Well, our Sunday dinner is missing," Ma broke in, "kettle and all. I reckon our thief has taken it, and left that brooch to pay for it."

"It must be worth a small fortune!" Pa said.

"I'd say so," Ma agreed. "Look at those rubies, sapphires, and emeralds sparkle!"

"And the gold's heavy, too," Pa said. "Our thieves must have plied their trade in some higher social circles before they came to Stoney Creek! But I reckon this more than pays for everything they've taken from us."

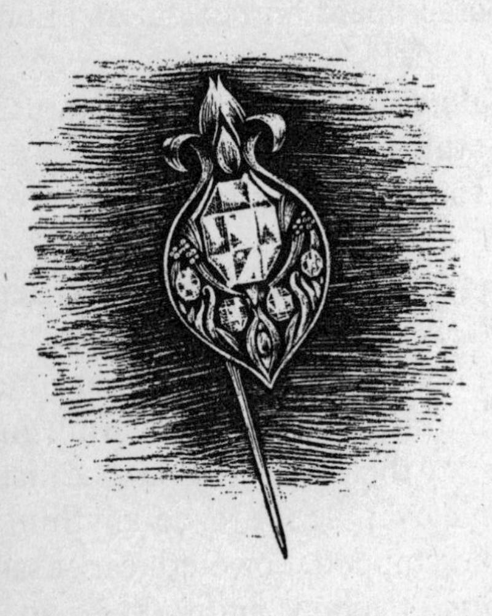

"We can't keep this brooch, Hiram!" Ma exclaimed in horror. "It must belong to somebody, somewhere! It wouldn't be right for us to keep it!"

"Well, Della, it looks like we have no choice at the moment," he said, "since we have no idea where it came from or who it may have belonged to once upon a time." He walked over to the mantel and dropped the brooch into a small bowl. "When we catch these thieves," he added, "we'll get answers to a lot of things, including our mysterious brooch."

That night and the next, Pa slept in his clothes. He left his gun propped against the wall by the bed, but no thief came to disturb their rest.

On Monday, Sarah enlisted Luke's help in making wooden paddles to be used as slates, and charcoal "pencils" made of sticks blackened in the fire. Carefully, she burned the letters of the alphabet into a large paddle, and numerals from one to ten into another. She asked permission to use Pa's Bible for a reading text. Now she had all the tools Mrs. Coomes had had to teach the school at Harrodstown.

What else should she do? She had studied with her cousins' tutors in Williamsburg, but, other than that poor example at the fort, she had never been inside a real school. She had read about them, though, and as she prepared a roster of students from which to call the roll, she vowed that her school would be the very best it could be.

If everybody who was eligible came, she would have six

students for her first school—the three middle Mackey boys, the two Willard brothers, and Jamie. She was excited, and in turn, terrified that she wouldn't be able to control the boys, that she would suddenly run out of things to teach, that the children simply would not come to school.

Pa had promised to see that she had enough wood to keep the fireplace going, now that November had turned toward winter. Maybe she could assign one of the bigger boys to tend the fire.

If only I had some children's books! Sarah thought again wistfully. She would send a letter to Uncle Ethan and ask him to send her some books, as soon as she could find someone who would carry her letter to the fort to be taken back East by the next traveler. It would take a long time though, and even longer for the books to be brought back.

First, she must teach them all the alphabet and simple arithmetic. She could do that with the examples she had made on Luke's wooden paddles. If any of her pupils already knew how to read and write, she would assign them readings from the Bible.

Tuesday dawned gray and cold, threatening rain, but Sarah refused to let the day dampen her spirits. She dressed herself and Jamie warmly, and they set off for the church building hand in hand.

When she opened the door, she was surprised to find that the room was already warm and cozy from a fire someone had built in the huge stone fireplace that took up most of the front wall. Even with the shutter closed over the one window at the side, the fire gave enough light to see the letters and numerals on the teacher's paddles she hung from the wooden mantel.

Soon her pupils began to arrive and sit down on the rough,

backless benches. When she called the roll, all six of them answered, "Present!"

"How many of you know your letters and your numbers?" she asked. No one raised his hand.

"I know how to write my name," Jamie volunteered proudly.

"I can count to ten, and I know a,b,c,d,e,f,g,h,i,j,k,lmnop," the oldest Willard boy, Will Junior, said. "Rachel taught me."

"Good!" Sarah praised. "Anybody else?" When no one else responded, she held up the alphabet paddle and began to teach them the first three letters.

By lunchtime, all of them could recite half of the alphabet, except the youngest Mackey boy. Caleb was nearly a year younger than Jamie, and she decided not to push him.

After they had eaten their lunches, consisting of everything from cold sweet potatoes to biscuits and ham, Sarah taught them the little song Malinda had taught her at the fort last year.

"As the deer panteth for the water brooks, so my soul longeth after Thee," she sang. "My soul thirsteth for God, for the living God."

Then Jamie had to tell them about the little deer asleep in the thicket beside his mother, the story Sarah had used when he was smaller to get him to sleep. Then more of the children wanted to share stories, and she let them. Before she knew it, the day was nearly over.

"I'll bank that fire for you, ma'am," David Mackey offered.

"Why, thank you, David," Sarah said. "Was it you who started the fire this morning?"

He shook his head. "No, ma'am. My big brother, Trace, built it this morning, but he didn't want you to know it. I will do it for you in the morning, though," he promised seriously.

"Do you know how to build a fire, David?" she asked

doubtfully. He really wasn't very big, only nine.

"Yes, ma'am. I build fires for my ma all the time. And I take out the ashes, too."

"All right, then," she agreed. "You can be my 'Keeper of the Fireplace,'" she said, and was surprised to see the little boy's usually solemn, freckled face split with a proud grin.

"I want to be something, too!" his seven-year-old brother, Samuel, begged. "I want to be keeper of something, too!"

Sarah racked her brain for some job the little boy could do that would make him feel as special as his big brother. Finally, she came up with, "You can be 'Keeper of the Water Bucket,'" she said.

His freckled face, a miniature copy of his brother's, fell. Sarah was afraid he was going to burst into tears.

"What's wrong, Sammy?" she asked in alarm. "You don't have to do it, if you don't want to." *Dear God,* she prayed silently, *please show me what to say!*

"It ain't that, ma'am. It's just that he can't lift a full bucket of water, yet," David explained.

Sarah refused to let herself laugh. She patted Samuel on the head. "Well, Samuel," she said, "who wants a full bucket of water to set around growing stale? You can bring us a good fresh half-bucket several times a day."

The little boy beamed up at her. "Yes, ma'am!" he said happily. "I'm your 'Keeper of the Water'!"

Then all the little boys began a clamor. "What can I be, Teacher? What can I be?"

Sarah sighed. Now that she had named two of them "keeper" of something, she supposed she'd have to give them all similar titles so none of them would feel left out. But what could she find for the rest of them to do?

"What can I be, Teacher?" Rob Willard asked again.

"You can be 'Keeper of the Wooden Paddles,' Rob," she said, thinking fast. "And Will Junior, you can be 'Keeper of the Charcoal Pencils.' That means you will have to keep them sharpened and blackened in the fire."

Will nodded. "I can do that, Teacher," he assured her.

Caleb Mackey was looking up at her expectantly. Sarah racked her brain for something the little boy could do. Finally, she came up with, "You can be 'Keeper of the Door,' Caleb. When anybody knocks, you may open the door and invite them into the schoolroom."

"What if it's an Indian?" Rob Willard asked.

"Indians don't knock, silly!" his brother, Will Junior, mocked. "They just barge right in and start bashing in heads with their tomahawks."

"Will!" Sarah scolded.

"Well, they do," the boy insisted. "That's what my pa says, and my pa knows all about Indians. He's fought 'em many a time."

"What can I be, Sarah?" Jamie interrupted. "Don't you have a job for me?"

"Oh, yes, of course I do, Jamie. I have a very important job for you," she answered, wondering what on earth it might be. Then she said, "You'll be the 'Keeper of Order,' and line up everybody according to size when we get a drink, go outside for recess or to be excused, or when we have our recitations."

Jamie thought about that for a moment, then he nodded. "All right," he agreed solemnly, throwing back his shoulders and sitting up very straight in his seat, as befitted his new position.

To hide her amusement, Sarah went to the window, opened the shutter, and looked out. "Boys, the sun is already sinking behind the hills," she said. "I know that almost all of you are big enough to walk home by yourselves, but I'm sure your parents don't want you walking at the edge of that forest in the dark." She fought off a shiver. She didn't like the idea, either.

"In fact," she added, "I think we should start school a little later in the morning, now that the days are growing shorter. We will come after the sun lights the path, and begin school at nine o'clock for the rest of our term."

With that, she shooed them all out of the classroom, shut the door and latched it, pulling the latchstring outside so they could open it in the morning.

It was nearly dark by the time Sarah and Jamie reached home. They ate supper by the light of two fat, yellow candles made of bear tallow, each taking turns telling about their first day of school. Sarah helped Ma clean up the supper dishes, then she headed off to bed.

Thoroughly exhausted from the challenge of meeting her new responsibilities, Sarah was sleeping soundly when she was awakened by the squawking of a chicken, the dogs' frantic barking, and the restless stamping of the horses.

She jumped out of bed and ran to the door of the cabin, just as Pa and Luke took off at a run for the barn. They were barely visible in the faint light of a few stars that, without the moon, had braved the black sky alone. Sarah could barely see the outline of the barn. Then the doors swung open, and Pa and Luke were swallowed up by the darkness inside.

"Take your hands off me!" Sarah heard a high-pitched voice scream. "Let go of me!"

She saw three dark figures come from the barn. One of them—she thought it was Luke—stopped to bar the barn door, then came back to help Pa force the third figure across the barn lot and into the yard.

★ Chapter Seven ★

"Please let me go!" their captive begged.

"Let you go?" Luke squawked. "You're lucky we didn't shoot you! You thief!"

"No! I'm not a thief!" The figure renewed its struggling. "Please let me go!"

"You're not a thief?" Pa said scornfully. "You just stole a couple of roosters, several gallons of milk, and who knows how many eggs from us!" he said, opening the gate and pulling his captive through. "And then there's the Larkins' cover and the Mackeys' bearskin."

"And, unless I miss my guess, that's the Mackey boy's breeches and shirt you've got on," Luke added. "His ma hung them out to dry after a washing and hasn't seen 'em since!"

"I didn't take those things! Just some food, and I tried to pay!" their captive insisted, struggling harder. "Please let me go!"

Sarah could see though that Pa kept a firm grip on one side and Luke on the other, propelling the struggling figure through the cabin door. She followed.

"For pity's sake!" Ma exclaimed. "He *is* just a child!"

The captive glared at them from dark eyes half-hidden under a tangled fall of dark hair that was covered with a man's shapeless hat.

Sarah almost laughed. So this was the dangerous thief she had feared would murder them in their sleep, this pathetic creature hardly taller than Jamie, with its knobby bones sticking out of the collar and cuffs of the oversized blue shirt!

"Where did you come from, boy?" Pa asked gruffly.

Their captive stared into the fire without speaking.

Ma went and knelt in front of the child. "How old are you?" she asked gently, "and where are your mother and father?"

Suddenly the child began to sob, swiping with one sleeve

at the tears that left tracks down its dirty cheeks. Ma reached up to smooth the dark hair out of the thin face. She removed the floppy hat, and Sarah gasped as a tangle of dark hair came cascading down over the captive's shoulders.

"Why, Hiram," Ma exclaimed, "it's a little girl!"

8

May the good Lord have mercy upon us!" Pa muttered, staring at the little girl before them.

"Child, tell us where your parents are, and we will take you home," Ma offered.

The child shook her head, sobbing so hard that Sarah could hardly understand the words she uttered. Finally, she understood, "Dead. Both dead."

"But where are you living?" Ma asked.

"I . . . I've got a place," the little girl said cautiously. "Please let me go!" she begged. "He needs me, and he'll be so worried if I don't come back soon. He didn't want me to come, but we were hungry, and . . ."

"Who, child?" Pa questioned. "Who will be worried?"

"And you tried to pay for what you took by leaving us your beautiful gold brooch," Ma interrupted. "Was it your mother's?"

The little girl nodded, tears again welling up in her eyes.

"You poor thing!" Ma said, and Sarah knew that soon Ma

would be feeding the dirty little creature. Sure enough, the next words out of Ma's mouth were, "Sarah, come help me fix this little waif something to eat."

The child continued to sniff and wipe away tears as she hungrily ate the cornbread Ma crumbled into a cup of milk. When she had finished, she jumped up from the table. "I'm sorry for all the trouble we've caused you," she said. "We were just so hungry, and the animal traps didn't work, and after he got . . . hurt, I knew I had to try to find food."

"Hurt?" Pa broke in. "You mean 'shot,' don't you?"

"No, I don't. I mean, I'm sorry!" the little girl repeated. "If you could just let me have some cornbread for Charlie and let me go, I promise you we will never bother you again!"

"Who is Charlie?" Pa asked. "Is he making you steal for him?"

"He's . . . nobody, and he's fine, really. Please just let me go." The little captive was in tears once again.

"You just stay here tonight, dear," Ma said soothingly, "and we'll see about getting you home in the morning."

The child studied each of them in turn, then, apparently without hope, sank down on the hearth and stared into the fire.

"Well, I hate to leave good company," Luke said yawning, "but we've got a long day ahead of us tomorrow. I'm going to bed."

Ma wet a clean cloth in warm water and handed it to the little girl. "Wash your face and hands, child, and I will find you a gown of some kind. You're smaller than Sarah, and bigger than Elizabeth, but we'll find something. What's your name, dear?"

"Katie," she muttered, still staring into the fire.

When Sarah finally went back to bed, Pa had moved Jamie, still sleeping soundly, into his and Ma's bed, and Katie, wearing one of Jamie's nightshirts, was tucked into the trundle bed beside Sarah and Elizabeth. This time, Sarah felt no need to keep watch, and in no time, she felt herself sinking into sleep.

When Sarah awoke, the sun was peeking in around the shutter, and the rooster was crowing. Memory came flooding back, and she raised up on one elbow to look at the little girl they had captured last night. But the trundle bed was empty, the covers spread over it neatly as though no one had slept there.

Quickly, Sarah dressed and went into the big room, where Ma was busy at the fireplace coaxing the fire to life from last night's coals.

"Where's Katie?" Sarah asked.

Ma looked up. "Isn't she in your room?"

Sarah shook her head. "When I awoke, her bed was empty."

Ma sighed. "She's gone, then, I reckon." She turned to the mantel above the fireplace. "I wasn't able to give her back her brooch," she said. Then Sarah followed Ma's gaze to the now empty spot where the cloth-covered cake of cornbread had set last night. "And I'm sure there will be a crock of milk missing from the springhouse, too," Ma said sadly.

"But, Ma, why did she steal our food and sneak out in the night? Why didn't she just ask? You're always willing to help."

"She didn't know that, Sarah." Ma shook her head. "Did you see the way she put away that cornbread mush last night? She was so hungry! And she was worried about someone she called Charlie. I don't doubt she's taking breakfast to him right now."

Sarah nodded. "Maybe she'll come back when she gets hungry."

"I doubt if we'll ever see her again," Ma said. "She'll probably move on now that she knows we've found her out."

"I guess you're right," Sarah agreed.

"It's cold out this morning, Sarah," Ma said then. "You and Jamie wrap up good." She sighed. "I just can't imagine how that little girl can survive out there in the woods now that the weather is turning cold," she said.

"Well, if she suffers, it was her choice," Sarah said. "She should have stayed here and let us help her."

Then Sarah pictured the little girl hungrily spooning up mush, wiping tears on her sleeve, her thin bones showing through her skin as she had slipped easily into the nightshirt of a five-year-old boy. She pictured her playing with the stick dolls in the playhouse, making a tiny bouquet for their table. All at once, Sarah felt tears gather in her throat. There had been something about Katie that touched her, in spite of the dirt and the thieving.

Suddenly, she knew what it was. The child's dark eyes had reminded her of Megan back in Williamsburg, though Katie's eyes held a sadness that Meggie had never known. Sarah supposed it was due to the death of her mother and father, and to the hardships she had known since then.

Sarah wrapped Ma's shawl around Jamie, over his heavy deerskin shirt, and threw her warm cloak over her dress. Even so, the damp wind chilled her as they walked through a thick, white fog that hung over the creek valley.

Where was Katie now? She must be staying nearby, or she wouldn't have been able to make off so freely with supplies from the homesteads along Stoney Creek. And she must be cold, wearing only that thin shirt she had taken from the Mackey clothesline, Sarah thought as she and Jamie entered the schoolroom.

To her surprise, again this morning, the classroom was warm and cozy with a good fire blazing in the fireplace and a supply of logs stacked neatly beside it. She had doubted that David would be able to fulfill his promise, but obviously he had, she thought, giving him a warm smile of approval.

As Sarah walked toward the front of the room, all three Mackey boys were in their seats, looking back at her with wide blue eyes, each one a freckled copy of the one next to him. There wasn't a smile among them, and she wondered what had happened to the mischievous grins they had had such a hard time keeping under control yesterday.

Then a creepy feeling on the back of her neck made Sarah turn and look at the back of the room. There, in the far corner of the back bench, sat Trace Mackey, his pale blue eyes challenging her to say anything about him being there.

She had seen the boy in church, always sitting in that same back corner, usually giving Rachel Willard glance for glance. He wasn't quite as tall as Luke, but certainly taller than she was, Sarah measured with her eyes, and his muscles strained the seams of his homespun shirt. She thought Ma had said he was about fifteen years old. What was he doing here in her class of four to nine year olds?

In her dreams of being a teacher, never once had this situation crossed her mind. Was Trace planning to stay and be a part of the class? What could she do if he caused trouble? Spank him?

She took a deep, steadying breath. "Good morning, Trace," she said. "Thank you for the fire. It feels good on a damp, foggy morning like this."

He had the palest blue eyes she had ever seen, almost like blue ice. His eyes never left hers as his mouth curved slightly in a half grin. "You're welcome, ma'am," he said.

Sarah couldn't be sure if he was just being polite, or if he was mocking her.

Just then, the door crashed open and the Willard boys tumbled in, scuffling over something, their red hair standing on end.

"Sit down, boys, and we will begin our lessons," Sarah said, beginning to feel a little desperate. There was more to teaching school, she thought, than helping little boys learn to read and figure!

Yesterday, the class had been well-behaved, and she had not even had to raise her voice to discipline them. She had expected the same today, but maybe it had been easier yesterday because everything was new to them and had held their interest. Maybe she wasn't going to be such a good teacher, after all, she thought nervously, feeling Trace's gaze still upon her as she spoke to the younger children.

Finally, she could stand it no longer. "Are you planning to be a part of this class, Trace?" she blurted.

His little brothers sat up straight, three more pairs of pale eyes watching her from freckled, copycat faces.

"Now, ma'am, do you think I look like one of these tadpoles waiting to learn how to swim?" he asked mockingly.

"Then why are you here?" she demanded, refusing to let him stare her down.

"Why, I came to build you a fire and to see what kind of teacher my little brothers have here," he answered innocently.

"Very well," she said, standing as straight and tall as she could, trying to seem as grown-up as possible. "But you needn't come back tomorrow. David says he can build the fire."

"Yes, ma'am!" Trace said, with a defiant grin and an icy flash of eyes. He leaned back against the wall behind his bench and folded his arms across his chest.

Sarah hurried into a recitation of the alphabet, then had the children count as Rob Willard handed out the wooden paddles. "One!" they sang out as he gave David his, and "Two!" as he handed one to Will Junior. "Four!" they said in unison, as he gave Sammie the third one. Sarah had to start all over with the number paddle, pointing out the number three and having the children copy the numerals one through ten on their own paddles.

Finally it was lunchtime, and Sarah helped the younger boys spread out the lunches they had brought. When she looked up again, Trace had disappeared. She walked to the window and looked out, then to the door, but there was no sign of him.

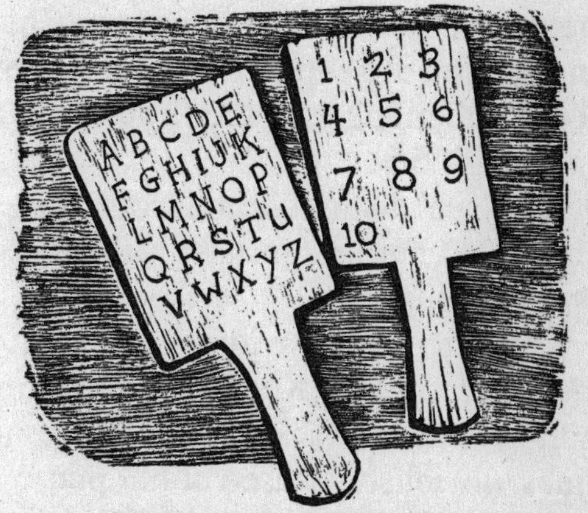

The fog had mostly blown away by now, but a sharp gust of wind came into the room as she stood with the door open, fanning the fire and causing the children to look back at her with questioning looks. Quickly, she shut the door, then barred it. She couldn't have said why, except that she felt better knowing no one could just walk in unannounced.

After lunch, Sarah read to her class from Pa's Bible, the story of little David, the shepherd boy who became king.

"Now, I want each of you to tell us a story of something that has happened to you since you moved to Kentucky," she said, "something that required you to show bravery in the face of danger, like David did when he faced the lion and the bear that attacked his sheep or the giant that threatened his people."

Every child, even little Caleb, had a story to tell, and she talked with them about how God had helped them in each situation.

With Trace not there to follow her every move with his mocking eyes, the afternoon passed quickly. The children performed their various chores at the end of the day without having to be told, the Willard boys neatly stacking the tablets and pencils on the front bench for the next day's use, Samuel Mackey emptying the water bucket so it would be ready to hold fresh water the next morning, his brother, David, banking the fire to keep it overnight and bringing in kindling and wood and piling it by the fireplace in readiness for Thursday morning's fire.

"It sure looks like rain out there," he explained, "and there ain't nothing so aggravating as trying to start a fire with wet kindling!"

"You're right, David," Sarah had to agree. "I'm glad I have such a dedicated Keeper of the Fire!" She smiled at him, and he grinned back at her, freckles disappearing into laugh lines, obviously pleased at her praise.

"Now, let's get home before dark sets in," she urged.

Trace was waiting for his brothers outside. "Goodnight, ma'am," he said, giving her a mocking grin and a sideways glance from those unnerving blue eyes.

"Goodnight," she answered, taking Jamie's hand and leading him quickly away down the path. "Please, God," she prayed silently, "don't let him come back to school anymore!"

"Well, Sary girl, how do you like being a teacher?" Pa asked that night, as they ate supper together in the glow of candles.

"I like it fine," she answered. "The children are well-behaved, for the most part." And she shared some stories of the red-haired Willard boys and the freckle-faced Mackeys.

"Trace Mackey came to school today," Jamie announced, popping the last bite of his third biscuit into his mouth. Apparently, going to school gave the little boy an appetite.

Ma frowned. "Trace Mackey? Isn't he a mite old for this school, Sarah?"

"Did he cause you trouble, Sary?" Pa asked. "If that rapscallion is causing you trouble, I'll go with you in the morning and take care of that young man!"

Sarah wished Jamie hadn't said anything about Trace. "He didn't cause trouble, Pa, but he *is* too old for a class of four to nine-year-olds, Ma. And he made me nervous, with those pale blue eyes of his watching everything I did. But he left at noon, and we didn't see him again until this afternoon when he met his brothers to walk them home."

"He probably was just curious about the school and its teacher," Ma said, "and since he's satisfied that curiosity, he probably won't be back."

"He'd better not!" Pa said, spearing a potato angrily with his fork. "You let me know, Sary, if he keeps hanging around."

Thursday morning, though, Sarah found Ma's prediction to be true. She almost wished it hadn't been, for there was no fire blazing on the hearth when they arrived at school, and the classroom was cold. It took both she and David to get a fire going, and they all huddled around it until mid-morning when the room began to feel warm.

Early that afternoon, David raised his hand. "Miss Sarah, may I be excused to bring in the wood for tomorrow?"

"Yes, David, go ahead," she said. "With that sky like it is, we may be in for the rain it's been promising. I'd like for us to get home before it starts."

That night, the rain did set in, a heavy pounding that wore itself into a steady drizzle by morning. Sarah really didn't want to go out in it, or take Jamie, but she hadn't told the children what to do if it rained. She'd have to be at school in case they came.

The wind-driven rain soon dampened her cloak, and she was wet and cold by the time she and Jamie had covered the two miles or so to the church building. No one else was there, so she began laying the fire herself.

Soon the Willards came in, wet and shivering, and went to stand by the fire to dry out.

David Mackey and his brothers followed, shaking rain from their deerskin coverings and hanging them on the wooden pegs the men had placed at the back of the room for the convenience of the churchgoers. Sarah saw David look at the fire she had started, but he said nothing.

That afternoon, when he brought in wood, he said, "We need a covering for that woodpile, Miss Sarah. This wood is soaked through."

"I'll see if Pa's got an extra deerskin we can throw over it until he can build us a woodshed," she promised. "And, class, if it is raining like this Monday morning, there will be no school."

By Saturday morning, though, the rain had stopped, and the sun was climbing the hill behind the cabin, kindling its own kind of fire in the reds, oranges, and yellows of the trees.

After morning chores were done, Sarah asked Ma if she could take Elizabeth and Jamie to gather hickory nuts.

"I don't want you out of sight of this cabin," Ma hesitated. "I know we don't have much to fear from our little thief, but you never know what's out there."

"I know, Ma, but there's a big old hickory tree behind the barn, just at the edge of the forest. Remember? Luke and Jamie and I have gathered nuts there before." She didn't add that their last visit to the hickory tree had ended with Indians attacking the cabin and nearly scalping Ma. The hickory tree had nothing to do with it, though, she reminded herself. They had just come home from having such a good time there and found the Indians in the yard.

"All right, Sarah, but be careful," Ma cautioned. "And be back in time for the noon meal."

"We will, Ma," she promised, taking a hickory-bark basket for herself and one for Jamie from the pegs on the wall, and calling the children to go with her.

They crossed the meadow behind the barn, Jamie running

ahead, then stopping to wait for them. Sarah smiled, remembering how not too long ago it had been Jamie toddling along beside her, like Elizabeth, stooping to examine every bright-colored leaf and bug.

Then they were at the hickory tree, and Sarah handed Jamie his basket. "Leave the hulls on, Jamie," she instructed, "and we can throw them into the fire at home and watch the pretty colors they make as they burn."

"I know, Sarah!" Jamie said. "I know how to do it."

Elizabeth held tightly to Sarah's hand, watching Jamie pick up the green and black nuts and throw them into his basket. "Pity!" she said, throwing a bright yellow leaf into Sarah's basket.

"Yes, it's pretty, sweets, but we aren't gathering leaves, just hickory nuts," Sarah said. "Here, let me show you."

When their baskets were full, Sarah stood up, stretched, and took a deep breath. Then she took another, and a shiver went down her spine. That was wood smoke she smelled, and they were too far from the house to smell anything from the fireplace! Was there an Indian campfire nearby? If so, with Elizabeth to carry, could she get them out of here before they were discovered?

"Jamie, we've got to go now," Sarah said softly, gathering Elizabeth into her arms. But Jamie didn't answer. She looked around, but he was nowhere in sight! He had been there just a moment ago. Fear traveled through her. Where was he?

"Jamie!" she called softly. "Come here! We have to go!" Still, no answer. Sarah's heart began to race. Where was he? Had he wandered off into the woods searching for pine cones to make animals for his farm? There were no pine trees near the cabin.

At the nearest stand of pine trees, though, there was no sign of a tow-headed little five-year-old boy. The scent of smoke was stronger, a bitter smell that stung Sarah's nostrils and burned her throat. Wherever that fire was, they were very close to it!

Afraid now even to call his name, Sarah searched the pine thicket for Jamie. Then she saw him, stooped down under a big pine tree, carefully selecting the biggest cones and placing them on top of the nuts in his basket.

"Jamie!" she hissed. He turned and looked at her, then he motioned for her to wait, and turned back to his pine cones.

Sarah looked around anxiously. The smell of smoke was so strong! Her eyes searched the surrounding forest and the outcropping of rock ahead. Then her gaze fell on a small opening in the face of the rocks just beyond the pines. A thin trail of black smoke filtered out of the cave's entrance.

As she watched, a small figure ran out of the cave, picked up a tree branch, and threw it into the smoke. Flames licked at the wood, then blazed up.

"Katie?" Sarah breathed. Instead of an Indian camp, had they stumbled on the hiding place of their nighttime visitor? Should she march boldly up to the cave and confront her?

Sarah felt Elizabeth lay her head on her shoulder, and glanced down to see her stick her thumb in her mouth, her eyelids drooping sleepily. She looked over at Jamie, still absorbed in collecting pine cones. She glanced at the sky. The sun was nearly at the top of the hill. It was time for the noon meal, and she had promised Ma they'd be home by then. She had better take the children home and deal with Katie later, now that she knew where to find her.

"Come along, Jamie," Sarah said quietly. "We promised Ma we would be back by noon, and we need to hurry if we're going to keep that promise."

"All right, Sarah," Jamie agreed. "I've got all the cows and horses I can carry anyway."

Sarah looked at his basket and saw that he had taken out some of the nuts to make room for pine cones, but she didn't have time to argue with him. They could gather hickory nuts another day.

Sarah carried Elizabeth and urged Jamie ahead of her as they made their way back down the hill to the edge of the forest. Jamie stopped every now and then to retrieve a pine cone that fell from his overflowing basket.

By the time they reached the cabin, Pa and Luke were there to eat. Sarah helped Ma take up the food and put it on the table, but her mind was still on Katie. The little girl was bound to be hungry, and cold if the way she was trying to build up that fire was any indication. Sarah hoped the little girl would let them help her now.

Ma seemed to read her thoughts. "I worry about that little girl out there in the forest," she said. "I wish we could find her. She said her parents were dead, but there must be somebody who would take her in—grandparents, an aunt or uncle, somebody! She could stay with us till we could send word back East."

Pa offered thanks for the food. Then he said, "You know I don't mind helping a needy child, Della, but all of us out here in the wilderness work hard. We build homes and plant and harvest food. We raise chickens, geese, cows, and hogs to add to the wild game we kill. I don't appreciate some ornery yahoos stealing my hard-earned provisions!"

"Katie's just a hungry little girl, Hiram!" Ma said.

"I think she's as much of a thief as the other one is, and a liar to boot," Luke put in, drying his face and hands on a towel. "I'm going over to Betsy's for supper, Ma," he added.

★ Chapter Nine ★

"Tell Ruthie to come over here and play with me!" Jamie yelled as Luke went out the door. "I can't take my whole farm over there," he finished saying to the shut door where Luke had been, then glared at the rest of the family for laughing at him.

Sarah set a steaming bowl of fried potatoes on the table beside the platter of sausage. "I believe our thief was this other person with her, and that Katie tried to pay back some of what he took by gathering persimmons for us."

"Those apples sure would have tasted good with this sausage," Pa said. "Nobody fixes apples like your ma!"

"I just stew them with some sugar and a little cinnamon and nutmeg," Ma said, embarrassed at the praise. "Oh, I will be glad when our apple trees are old enough to bear fruit, and we don't have to depend on getting a few now and then from peddlers at the fort!"

"Well, we still have some of those persimmon preserves, don't we?" Pa asked sarcastically. "I guess I've eaten worse things, but I've sure had better!"

Ma grinned and slapped at his arm with the pot holder she had picked up to pull the biscuit pan out of the fireplace. "At least the child tried to pay her way," she said. "I worry about her out there in that wilderness with nobody to care for her."

"I've tried to find her," Pa admitted, "but they've either gone to ground like a pair of foxes with the dogs after 'em, or they've gone clean out of the area. But remember that whoever is with this 'hungry child' may be dangerous. You know, a lot of criminals have come west to keep from being prosecuted for their crimes back in the eastern colonies. This little girl's companion may be one of them."

"States, Pa," Sarah corrected. "Uncle Ethan and his friends

in Williamsburg would never let any of us call them colonies any more. He always said, 'We're not the colonial possession of any foreign power. We are the United States of America!'"

"I know, Sary," Pa said. "That's what this war your brother Nate and your Uncle Ethan are fighting is all about, to make us free of England's rule. And they say the British are paying the Indians for Kentucky settlers' scalps, so I'm not any too fond of the redcoats, either." He forked a big bite of sausage and potatoes into his mouth and chewed.

"Anyway, as I was saying, many criminals from the eastern *states,*" he raised one eyebrow at Sarah, "have come out here to escape the consequences of their crimes. If this deadbeat with Katie is one of them, he could be extremely dangerous."

So far, Pa had just warned them to be careful. He hadn't said anything about staying close to the cabin, Sarah thought with relief, for she aimed to go after Katie as soon as she got a chance.

About mid-afternoon, there was a knock on the door, and a voice called, "It's Rowena, Della!"

Jamie ran to the door and threw it open, and Mrs. Larkin and Ruthie came into the cabin.

Jamie drew Ruthie over to his farm, then began to tell her about his new school. He rearranged his farm into a schoolroom, using his pine cones for children instead of cows and horses.

"I wish I could go to school," Sarah heard Ruthie say.

Why not? Sarah thought. *Girls can learn just as well as boys can. . . .*

"Betsy's helping out at the Mackey place today, or she'd have come with us, Sarah," Mrs. Larkin interrupted Sarah's thoughts. "The Mackey baby has been sick, and Anna has her hands full with all those boys and no girl to help her, and another one on the way! I tell you, Della, I just dread the thought of giving up my Betsy, though I know Luke will make her a good husband."

"Has Luke spoken to Mark?" Ma asked warily.

"He didn't tell you? That's a male for you!" Mrs. Larkin laughed. "Luke asked Mark for Betsy's hand last Sunday afternoon. They're planning a spring wedding. You don't mind, do you, Della?"

"Oh, no!" Ma hastened to assure her. "Betsy's my idea of a perfect daughter-in-law. I thought that rascal Luke had plans, for he's been talking about where he'd like to build a cabin, but he's never said why or when."

"I reckon boys are like that," Mrs. Larkin said. "Betsy wants you to stand up with her, Sarah, if you will," she added.

"I'd be proud to stand up with Betsy when she marries my brother," Sarah said. "You tell her I want to hear all about it."

Mrs. Larkin nodded. Then she sighed, and Sarah was surprised to see tears gather in the woman's blue eyes, so like Betsy's. "Betsy will be fifteen by spring, the same age I was when I married Mark," she said. "And she and Luke will make a good couple. It's just that . . ."

"I know how you feel, Rowena," Ma said sympathetically. "I could hardly stand for Sarah to go to Williamsburg, even though I knew it was for her good. But Betsy and Luke will be living close by, and you know how newlyweds are. They'll probably be at your house for dinner one Sunday and mine the next!"

As the women chatted companionably, Sarah suddenly felt shut out and alone. She really had no one with whom she could talk and laugh like that. Betsy's thoughts were no longer those of a girl, but had become the hopes and dreams of a woman, as Tabitha's had been. She wished Megan were here. Even though the little girl had been five years younger, Sarah had enjoyed her company a lot.

Picturing Megan's dark eyes suddenly reminded her of

Katie. "Ma, may I go for a walk?" she asked. "Elizabeth's taking her nap, and Jamie's busy with Ruthie. I won't be gone long."

At Ma's nod, Sarah was out the door before she could recall Pa's warning and change her mind. She was nearly to the woods when she remembered she had meant to bring food for Katie, but maybe she would be able to persuade the little girl to come home with her.

Sarah stopped to locate the green boughs of the pines among the brightly colored trees, then plunged into the woods. Soon she stood before the opening in the rocks. She peered inside.

"Katie?" she called softly.

"What do you want?" a gruff, male voice answered.

Sarah tried to see inside the dim cave, but her eyes were blinded by the outside light. "I . . . I'm looking for a little girl named Katie," she stammered. "Is she here?"

"What do you want with her?" the voice growled.

"We caught her trying to steal food the other night. Then she ran away, and I'm concerned about her being hungry and cold," Sarah answered honestly.

"It's none of your concern," he said. "Now get on out of here and leave us be!"

Not knowing what else to do, Sarah turned to go and saw Katie standing just out of sight of the opening to the cave. She motioned for Sarah, and Sarah went to her.

"Katie, are you all right?" she asked. "And who is that man in the cave?"

Katie's dark eyes studied her seriously, then she sighed. "He's my brother, Charles. Ma took sick soon after the soldiers took our pa away. When she was dying, she made Charlie promise to take care of me. Afterwards, they made us leave our house with only what we could carry on our backs. Charlie and I have just wandered since then. We were doing fine, too, until—"

"Doing fine?" Sarah interrupted. "Do you call stealing food and living in a miserable cave doing fine?"

Katie looked down at her feet, which showed through torn places on her shoes. "We ran out of bullets to kill game, and the traps didn't work. Then Charlie started stealing food for us. But since he got shot the other night, he's not been able to hunt for food."

"So Pa *did* shoot him!" Sarah exclaimed. "And now you're having to steal for him."

"I tried to feed us on berries and greens," she said, "but there's not much out there now. That's why I was at your place trying to get a chicken. I thought chicken soup would give him strength. Ma always fixed us chicken soup when we were sick."

★ Chapter Ten ★

"Come home with me, Katie," Sarah urged. "My ma will feed you and fix your clothes, and you will have a dry, warm place to sleep, and we can take care of Charlie. Then we can hunt for any relatives you might have back East, your grandparents or aunts and uncles."

"No!" Katie said. "We were Tories. Everybody hated us. We have nobody, and Charlie needs me. I won't leave him!"

Tories! The hated word tore through Sarah like a knife. The Tories, colonists who were loyal to King George, fought with the redcoated army of England against her brother, Nathan, and the Patriot army. They had put her Uncle Ethan in prison and tortured him. Surely the Tories deserved hating! But could she hate this hungry, dirty child who had nobody?

"We'll take your brother with us," Sarah repeated. "No harm will come to him. Ma will make him well."

Katie was shaking her head. "He's too weak to walk, and he's burning up with fever. Sometimes . . ."

"Katie, listen to me," Sarah begged. "You're brother needs medical attention. People die from untended bullet wounds!"

Suddenly, the little girl began to cry, wiping tears away with the sleeve of her stolen shirt. "I know he needs a doctor, but he won't hear to it," she sobbed. "If we just had some food, we'd be all right. I know we would!"

Sarah was beside her with her arms around her before she knew she had moved. "Don't cry, Katie. Just let me get my pa and my brother to move Charlie to our house where my ma can doctor him," she coaxed. "She's as good as any doctor, and she's got all kinds of herbs and medicines. She can have your brother well again in no time, if anybody can." Sarah pushed aside the thought that he was a Tory. He was a human being, and he needed help. She was sure Ma would see it that way, too.

Katie stepped back and looked into Sarah's eyes, as though trying to decide if she should trust her.

"Katherine Louise!" a voice croaked from the cave. "Don't you dare let anybody come here! Do you hear me?"

Determination hardened on Katie's face. "Please, lady, just bring us some food, and don't let anybody know where we are!"

As she looked into the dark, pleading eyes, all at once Sarah felt her heart melt. "All right, Katie. My name is Sarah, remember? And I will bring you some food, but if your brother isn't better very soon, you must let my ma doctor him."

"Just get us some food, and we'll be all right," the little girl repeated.

Sarah got back to the cabin just as Mrs. Larkin and Ruthie were leaving. Ma and Jamie had come outside with them.

Sarah grabbed some cold biscuits and a few uncooked sweet potatoes, put them in a small basket, and covered them with a cloth. She grabbed the deerskin bottle Pa had given her to carry water on the trip home, and she looked around for an extra cover, but there was none. Then her gaze fell on her cloak. She snatched it off the peg and ran out of the room.

Ma and Jamie came into the cabin, and Sarah quickly covered the basket with her cloak.

Jamie went back to his corncobs and started rearranging them from a schoolroom to a farm again. "Girls don't know a thing about schooling or farming!" he muttered, as though he hadn't been delighted to play with Ruthie all afternoon.

"Where are you going, Sarah?" Ma asked, eyeing the cloak. "It's getting late to be wandering around outside."

"I just thought I would . . . ah . . . gather the eggs," Sarah answered, giving her a quick glance at the basket, but not long enough for Ma to see that it already held something. She threw the cloak around her shoulders. "It's getting a little chilly out."

Ma looked at her for a moment, then turned to throw a fresh log on the embers of the fire. "I suppose you're right. I was so wrapped up in saying good-bye to our company, I didn't notice."

Jamie looked up. "Sarah, could Ruthie come to school with us? She wants . . ." He stopped, seeing that Sarah was dressed to go out. "Can I . . ." he began, but Sarah left the cabin and shut the door behind her before he could finish asking to go with her.

She ran to the barn, took four eggs from the hens' nests, and put them in her basket. She'd have to hurry back and gather the rest before Ma missed her.

A deep guilt came over Sarah. How awful to steal, and from her own family! Those eggs belonged to all of them. "I just won't eat eggs for a couple of days to make up for these," she vowed, as she hurried to the springhouse. "And I won't drink milk tonight for supper or in the morning for breakfast," she added, as she filled the deerskin bottle with milk from the crock in the spring.

Sarah knew Ma would send food to Katie if she asked, but she had promised not to let anybody know.

"Why do I always get myself between a rock and a hard place?" she muttered, as she walked rapidly toward the forest and the cave.

At the cave's entrance, she called, "Katie! It's Sarah!"

"I'm here, Sarah," Katie called from inside the cave. "I'm putting cold, wet cloths on Charlie's head to bring down the fever. That's what Ma always did."

Katie removed the cloth from her brother's head and plunged it into a bowl of water beside her. "Did you bring any chicken soup? Ma always fed us chicken soup when we were sick, but maybe that was for a cold and not a fever. Oh, I wish Ma was here!"

"We didn't have any chicken soup, Katie. I brought eggs and sweet potatoes and some cold biscuits. It was all I could find without telling Ma what I was doing."

Sarah's eyes were adjusting now to the dimness inside the cave, and she could see that the opening in the rock formed a small, round room. A meager pile of dry wood was stacked at one side, near the fire. Beside it sat Ma's kettle.

At the back of the cave, lying on a bearskin and covered with a woven cover, was a young man about Luke's size, his dark hair, much like Katie's, falling over his forehead in a tangle, his eyes glazed with the look of fever. As Sarah watched, he began to thrash around, throwing off the cover and mumbling words she could not understand.

"His fever has heated this water just like a fire!" Katie exclaimed. "I'll have to go to the spring for more."

"I'll go," Sarah offered. "Where is the spring?"

Katie pointed from the cave's opening, and Sarah grabbed the bowl, emptying it as she ran. When she got back, Charlie was shivering and Katie was trying to fold the cover to make it do the work of two.

Sarah whipped off her heavy cloak and placed it over the shaking boy. Still, the shaking continued. She could hear his teeth chattering. Suddenly, remembering the hot bricks they had used to keep their feet warm in the carriages of Williamsburg, Sarah grabbed the cloth from her basket, raked a hot rock from beside the fire with her shoe, and wrapped it in the cloth. She tucked the warm bundle under the covers at Charlie's feet. Still, he shook for several minutes before the chill began to ease.

★ Chapter Ten ★

"Katie, please let me get my ma to doctor him!" Sarah begged. "Your brother is very sick, and I don't know what to do for him. If the bullet is still in him, he could die from poisoning."

"No!" Katie yelled, stamping her foot. "No, he will not die!" She began to sob.

Sarah took hold of the little girl's shaking shoulders with both hands. "Look at me, Katie," she said. "No matter how much you love your brother, that love cannot keep him alive if he doesn't get the care he needs. I know you're doing all you can, but he needs medical attention. Please let Ma try to help him!"

Katie looked at her from troubled, tear-filled eyes. Then she shook her head no. "I promised Charlie," she said, the tears spilling down her cheeks.

Sadly, Sarah turned and left the cave, promising herself she would try again tomorrow after church.

I hear this traveling preacher is a young one," Pa said as they walked toward the churchyard Sunday morning. "They say he was a soldier on the battlefield when he got the call to preach."

"Was he a Patriot soldier, Pa?" Sarah asked. She wrapped her shawl around her, thinking with longing of the cloak she had left at the cave yesterday. She would try to help Katie and her brother, even if they had been Tories, but that was about as far as she was willing to go, with her brother and her uncle both fighting on the other side.

"I reckon he was," Pa answered. "He's a Virginian, and Virginia is a hotbed of patriotism, every bit as determined to be free from England as Massachusetts is, where the first shots in this war were fired."

"I don't know about all of Virginia, but almost everybody in Williamsburg is a Patriot," Sarah agreed. "What part of Virginia is this preacher from?"

"I don't know. Virginia's all I heard," he answered.

"Pa, there's something I want to discuss with you," she said then, changing the subject. "Little Ruthie Larkin wants to go to school in the worst way, and I was wondering why she couldn't join our class." All night, Sarah had been thinking about Ruthie's wistful comment as Jamie had told her about school, and she saw no reason why the little girl couldn't go to school.

"Sarah, that's unheard of!" Ma gasped. "You know that even in the capital city of Williamsburg, girls don't go to school. They learn at home, or have tutors."

"I know that, Ma. But why can't Ruthie learn to read and write along with Jamie? They play together all the time. What's so terrible about them going to school to- gether? What girls learn at home is not the same as what the boys learn at school."

"Girls learn what they need to know to be good wives and mothers, Sarah," Ma insisted.

"Yes, but learning to cook and sew and how to practice the social graces is not the same as learning Latin and history, geography and law. You know I've always been a better scholar than Luke, but until I went to Williamsburg, I never had the opportunity to study those advanced subjects, and then it was only because I had a tutor who offered them to me."

"What do you mean you're a better scholar than I am?" Luke asked belligerently.

Pa laughed. "I'm afraid she's got you there, son," he said. "You do a number of things better than Sary does—cut wood, hunt, shoot—but scholarship isn't one of them."

"But Ruthie is the only little girl of school age around here. She'd be the only girl among all those rough and tumble boys," Ma said doubtfully.

"I'd be there, Ma. And soon Elizabeth will be old enough to start school. Who knows how many little girls may move here in the future."

They were coming into the churchyard, and Sarah knew her time for persuading was up. "Pa, will you ask the others what they think about it?"

"We'll see," was all he would say, as he left them at the door of the church to take his seat with the other men.

Sarah had no sooner seated herself on the bench beside Ma and Elizabeth when there was a flurry of excitement at the back of the church. She assumed the preacher had arrived, but she vowed she would not turn to gawk at him like some country bumpkin.

As the young man passed her seat, Sarah saw that he wore a black coat and knee breeches over white stockings. His brown hair, about the color of Luke's, was tied back with a narrow, black ribbon. As he turned to face the congregation, she saw that the modest ruffles of his white shirt were starched, with a black ribbon tied at the throat.

Her eyes traveled upward past the smile that spread past his generous mouth and lit up his deep blue eyes. Then she gasped. She could feel her face flaming with color as she recognized the preacher. It was the young man she had first met as he waited on her in Greenhow's Store when she first moved to Williamsburg, and the young Patriot soldier she last had seen staring after her as she fled from the Governor's Ball!

He had asked her to dance, and caught up in the drama of that awful slave owner reclaiming her friend Marcus's wife as his slave, she had brushed him off rudely. She had hoped never to see him again, for the very memory of her rudeness caused her to burn all over with shame.

Now, here he stood before her, ready to conduct the

worship service in her home church! She never had known the young man's name, but she knew, beyond the shadow of a doubt, that here he stood!

It was all well and good that the young man had accepted God's call to preach, but why did he have to come here? Sarah agonized, slumping down to hide her red face behind Mrs. Strausberg's black straw hat.

"Ladies and gentlemen," he began in an unexpectedly deep, compelling voice, "please do not judge me by my youth, but give me a chance to share with you the experiences that have led—nay, forced!—me to ride the trails proclaiming the wrath of my God and extolling His tender mercies."

Soon, Sarah forgot her embarrassment, caught up in the intensity of his voice and the fervor of his words as he told of what he had seen on the battlefields of Virginia and Maryland.

"One day, I found myself in one of the fiercest battles possible to imagine," he continued. "We were surrounded by redcoats on every side. Many of our comrades had already fallen. There seemed no way out, and I began to pray.

"Suddenly, as plain as I would hear one of you speaking to me this morning, I heard a voice say, 'Jeremy Justice, I have battles for you to fight that are not of this world. You and the men with you will be spared this day.' Immed- iately, I fell flat on my face in the mud. 'Lord God,' I prayed, 'show me Your way, and I will follow it.'

"When I raised myself and looked around, I saw beings of brilliant white light pick up the weapons of my fallen comrades and drive the enemy back. I supposed they were angels. Anyway, I picked up my gun, walked off that field, and never looked back.

"This same God who called me from my worldly endeavors today calls you to accept the gift of His only Son, sent to die for your sins," the preacher continued, looking directly into the eyes of the congregation, one-by-one. "How shall you escape if you neglect so great a salvation?"

As his voice faded, the silence in the church was so thick Sarah thought she might smother in it. Then someone in the back of the room moaned as though in great distress. Someone else began to sob, quietly at first, then with growing intensity. Mrs. Strausberg fell to her knees and began to pray for mercy.

Exposed to view by Mrs. Strausberg's sudden defection, Sarah was horrified to find that the preacher's intense blue gaze met hers for an instant. She prayed that he would not recognize her.

All around her, people were caught up in repentance, crying out for mercy. Sarah had never seen anything like it at the church back in Williamsburg, or even at the little church in Miller's Forks. The services there had been quiet and dignified. What was it about this preacher that called forth such emotion?

Mr. Willard and his wife stood up and left the church with their two red-haired boys, but their daughter stayed in her seat, her green eyes fixed on the preacher, until her father came back and dragged her away by the hand.

As the service wound down, the preacher took a seat on the front bench, and Mr. Larkin walked down front.

"Preacher, you have been invited to have dinner with the Strausbergs today," he said, waving his hand in their general direction. "Folks, I think you've all heard by now that the Moores have discovered the identity of our thief, and it looks as if we have nothing to fear from her, so if there is nothing further to come before us this morning, let me remind you that Brother Justice will be back with us four weeks from now.

Meanwhile, we will have our usual services on Sunday, and our new school will continue here tomorrow morning at nine o'clock."

Sarah saw the preacher hold up his hand and stand up. "I want to commend you for starting your school," he said. "The church building stands empty six days of the week. To what better use could it be put than the education of our children?"

Sarah held her breath. "Please, Pa, ask them about Ruthie!" she urged silently.

"Why can't Ruthie go to school with me?" Jamie called out suddenly. "She wants to go. And she's my bestest friend. Sarah likes Ruthie, too. She won't mind if she comes to school."

Jamie looked over at Sarah as Pa whispered something in his ear. Sarah nodded and smiled at the little boy. Obviously, he had put a lot of thought into his speech. Sarah felt she had to back up what he had said.

"I'd be happy to have Ruthie in our class," she assured the congregation, returning Ruthie's shy, gap-toothed smile.

A buzz of startled reaction swept over the room, and Sarah heard one indignant "unheard of" comment. She saw Mrs. Mackey lean out across the aisle and whisper something to her husband.

"Hiram, would you take over here," Mr. Larkin said. "Since this conversation seems to center around my daughter, I don't think I'm the one to lead it."

Pa took Mr. Larkin's place down front and called on Mr. Mackey, who was standing by his bench.

"The missus and I are very pleased with what our boys have learned so far in this school. Davy and Sammy both know all their letters and are beginning to write words and do some figuring. Even little Caleb here can write his name and count to ten. None of them knew any of that until Sarah started teaching them. If she wants Ruthie Larkin to go to school, that's good enough for me."

"I think ve agree," Mr. Strausberg said, "don't ve, Mama?"

"I haf never heard of such a ting," his wife said, "but den everyting is different out here in de vilderness. Maybe it is time little girls vent to school." The black flower on her hat nodded vigorously.

"What do you think, preacher?" someone called from the back of the room.

"I'm afraid I agree with Mrs. Strausberg," he said, giving her a warm smile. "The harsh reality of life out here requires that many social graces be ignored and old traditions be broken. Why can't sending only little boys to school be one of them? Why can't the school on Stoney Creek be the one to make history by allowing little girls to attend?"

His smile this time was for Sarah, and she could feel her face turning red.

"Does anybody object to little Ruthie Larkin coming to school?" Pa asked. When there was no response, he said. "All right, then. I reckon Ruthie can join your class, Sary, if Rowena and Mark want her to."

"She has begged to go to school all this past week. She'll be ready tomorrow morning, if you could stop by for her on your way," Mrs. Larkin assured Sarah. Sarah nodded.

As the people got up and either made their way down front to talk with the preacher or to the back to leave, Sarah hesitated, torn between the desire to talk with this strange young man and the wish to escape before he could recognize her as the rude young woman he had asked to dance last Christmas.

She decided on escape, but she was too late. The preacher stood before her.

"Hello, there!" he said. "I haven't seen you since the night of the Governor's Ball, when you ran away from me like the devil himself was after you!"

Sarah stammered a greeting, then added, "I . . . I'm sorry!"

"Oh, don't be sorry, Sarah," the young man said. "But please tell me what I did that night to upset you so! I've wondered all these many months."

Sarah felt her face flush again, but she managed to tell him about Dulcie and her distress, and to apologize, again, for her rudeness. "It really had nothing to do with you, Sir," she assured him.

"I'm glad to hear it!" he said, with a grin that lit his whole face. "Perhaps we can discuss it in greater detail the next time I'm here."

With that, he went to join the Strausbergs, leaving Sarah standing in the churchyard, wishing the ground would open up and swallow her, wishing she had stayed at home today, wishing the Moores had been the ones to volunteer to feed the visiting preacher.

When the Moore family got back to the cabin after church, Katie was waiting for them at the gate.

"He's worse, lady," she said to Sarah. "He thinks I'm Ma. I can't get the fever down. Please help us!"

"Pa, Katie's brother is in bad shape," Sarah explained. "He's been shot, and he's out of his head with fever. Could we bring him here for Ma to doctor? They've been hiding out in a cave, near the pine thicket."

"He's been shot, you say?" Pa asked. "Then he must have been the thief we surprised in the barn that night. I thought I hit him!"

"Of course, I'll doctor him!" Ma said. "Hiram, you and Luke go get him, and I'll have things ready. I suspect there's a bullet that needs to come out."

"He may not come willingly," Pa said.

"He won't be able to put up much of a fight, but he will need to be carried," Sarah said. "He's too weak to walk."

"Luke, go hitch Bess to the small sled," Pa ordered. "We'll take it as close to the rocks as we can."

"If that cave is just above the pine thicket, I know about where it is," Luke said. "We can take the sled up as far as we've cut the road to haul wood."

"Why can't you take it all the way?" Sarah asked.

"Beyond that, the trees grow too close together for us to get the sled through," Luke answered impatiently. "Don't you remember anything about the wilderness, Sarah?"

"I'll rig up a stretcher so we can carry him down the hillside," Pa said. "Two of those poles we've cut for fencing and a deer hide should do it."

"Pa, it might be best if Katie went along to persuade her brother," Sarah said. "I'll go with her."

"All right, Sary," he answered. "Let's get going. It'll be dark before we know it."

In no time, Pa was riding Bess into the forest, with Luke, Sarah, Katie, and the stretcher on the sled behind them.

When they reached the last stand of trees where Pa and Luke had been cutting wood, they parked the sled and tied Bess's reins to a tree limb. Carrying the stretcher, Pa and Luke strode off through the trees, with Sarah almost running to keep up with them.

"There's the pine thicket," Luke said finally.

"The cave's right over there," Sarah pointed out, arriving breathless beside them.

"Hello, you there in the cave!" Pa called. "We've come to help you."

"It's me, Charlie!" Katie called reassuringly. There was no answer.

Pa went into the cave. Luke dropped the stretcher at the entrance and followed him.

★ Chapter Twelve ★

Standing in the doorway with her arm around Katie, Sarah heard, "Leave me alone!" Then there was a terrible scream, cut off abruptly. Katie gasped and began to cry.

"He's fainted!" That was Luke's voice.

"From the pain when we tried to move him," Pa explained. "But being unconscious will make it easier on him as we carry him."

Soon the two of them emerged from the cave with a limp, thin figure between them. They laid him on the stretcher, picked it up, and started down the hillside.

"Come along, Sarah, and bring the little girl," Pa called over his shoulder.

"Do you need to get anything from the cave, Katie?" Sarah asked.

Katie nodded and disappeared inside. In a moment, she was back with Ma's kettle, Sarah's cloak, and a small bundle tied up in a shawl. "It's all I could carry when we left the house," she explained, "some things that were my ma's."

Sarah took the kettle and the cloak, and they caught up with Pa and Luke as they were putting Charlie on the sled for the rest of the journey.

"Put him there on the table," Ma ordered when they came into the cabin with the unconscious young man on the stretcher.

Pa and Luke transferred the patient to the covered table, and Ma studied him.

"It's his leg, this one," Katie said, pointing. Then she added, "His name is Charlie. He's my brother."

Ma nodded and began cutting away his breeches above his right thigh. She grimaced as she saw the wound, festered and angry-looking. She poured something over it, then began to work. Charlie moaned some, but remained unconscious as

Ma cut and swabbed and probed.

Finally, Ma triumphantly held up a bullet for them all to see. Then she poured lavender water into the wound to cleanse it and wrapped a clean strip of cloth around it. "Put him on that pallet I fixed there by the fire, Hiram," she ordered.

After they had eaten a late meal and cleared away the dishes, Ma said, "Katie can sleep in Jamie's trundle bed beside Sarah and Elizabeth, and Jamie can go upstairs with Luke."

"All right!" Luke said, stooping down in front of Jamie. "Climb on my back, fellow, and you've got your own horse to ride to bed!" Giggling, Jamie obeyed and rode off slapping Luke on the shoulder, saying, "Giddy-up!"

Pa picked up Elizabeth, who had fallen asleep on the hearth rug, and carried her to the big bed in the other room. Then he came back and climbed into the bed in the corner of the big room. Ma, still dressed, was checking her patient.

"Aren't you going to bed, Ma?" Sarah asked as she helped Katie clean up and prepare for bed.

"I'm going to watch him for a while," she said, taking a seat in the high-backed rocking chair Pa had made her while Sarah was gone. "His fever is still pretty high, and I want to be sure he doesn't damage the wound in his delirium."

When Sarah awoke the next morning, Ma was still there, rocking slightly, but sound asleep, her head resting against the back of the chair. Her patient slept peacefully on his pallet by the hearth. Sarah touched his forehead, and found it still warm, but not burning to the touch.

"Ma!" she whispered. "His fever is down some. Go lie down a while, and I'll start breakfast."

Ma smiled at her gratefully. "I believe I will, Sarah. Thank you." She crossed the room and fell into bed in her clothes.

Pa and Luke came back from the barn, ate breakfast, and went back out. Still Ma slept, and Sarah did not have the heart to wake her. Finally, as Jamie came down the stairs clamoring for breakfast, Ma sat up and rubbed her eyes. She got up and went to her patient, touched his forehead, and smiled in satisfaction.

Katie appeared in the bedroom doorway, holding Elizabeth by the hand. She had dressed again in her stolen breeches and blue shirt, and had made an attempt to comb her tangled curls. "Is Charlie all right?" she asked anxiously.

"He's much better," Sarah told her. "Come have some breakfast. Elizabeth, I'll dress you after we eat," she added.

Katie had to go touch Charlie before she was satisfied. She came back and sat at the table with Sarah, Ma, Jamie, and Elizabeth. Sarah was amazed at the amount of food the child piled on her plate, but she ate it all and passed her plate for more!

"We're going to have to do something about some clothes for you, Katie," Ma said. "These boy's things just won't do for a young lady like you, and they're sadly in need of a good washing."

"I outgrew my dress," Katie mumbled around a mouthful of biscuit. "Charlie got me these things, I suppose from somebody's wash hung out to dry."

"Well, I'm sure Samuel Mackey will be glad to have them back," Ma said with a tired grin. "Katie, we can't just go around taking other people's things simply because we don't have any."

"I know," Katie admitted. "Our Ma taught us all about 'Thou shalt not steal' and how we should respect other people's property. I never stole anything in my life until I took your apples, and I tried to pay for them with those old persimmons. It was all I had. Charlie never stole anything, either," she added quickly, "until we got so desperate. There just didn't seem to be any other way to survive out here!"

"Child, if you had come and asked, any family on Stoney Creek would have helped you," Ma said. "But that's water over the dam, I reckon. Now, what are we going to do for a dress for you?"

"That brown dress Abigail gave me is a bit tight on me and more than a bit too short," Sarah offered. "Maybe you could make it fit Katie, Ma."

"Let her try it on, then," Ma agreed, reaching for her sewing box.

When Katie stood before them, the brown dress hanging from her thin frame and dragging on the floor, Ma walked around her with a frown on her face. "Hmmmm," she said.

★ Chapter Twelve ★

"With a tuck here and there, and with a new deep hem, I think this will do. Take it off, Katie, and don't put those filthy things back on. You've got to have a good bath and wash that hair, child."

"I had a bath," Katie protested.

Sarah raised her eyebrows. "When? Last summer?"

Katie ducked her head. "It was a nice hot day," she admitted.

"Well, Miss Katie, if you're going to share a room with Elizabeth and me, you've got to have another one, and soon!" Sarah said, with a smile to soften her words. "I've had about all I can stand of wood smoke mixed with old grease and a few other things I'd hate to try to identify!"

Katie looked back at Sarah sullenly. Finally, she grinned a crooked half grin. "I've lived with those smells so long, I reckon I just don't notice them anymore. If Ma was here, though, she'd say the same thing." Then she shivered. "I dread to think about getting in that cold creek!" she said.

Ma bit off a thread. "I've got a kettle of water already hot here over the fire. I was planning to wash a few things, but you can have the first kettleful for your bath, and you can take it in the bedroom," Ma promised. "It's a sight warmer than that creek!"

So, with a good bit of splashing and ducking, Sarah helped Katie take a bath and wash her hair. For want of something better, she gave her Jamie's nightshirt to wear until Ma could get the brown dress ready for her.

"Sit here on the hearth, Katie," she said then. "We're not starting school until nine o'clock, so I'll have time to brush your hair dry before we leave."

As she brushed the long, dark hair, watching it spring back into curls as it dried, Sarah was reminded of the countless times she had done the same thing for Megan. It was amazing, she thought, how much Katie looked like Megan. She had the same dark hair and eyes and was about the same height, though she was a great deal thinner. She was less talkative, too, with an underlying sorrow in her eyes that Sarah hoped Meggie would never know.

Katie smiled up at her. "My ma used to do this for me," she said dreamily, the firelight shining in her eyes.

Sarah gave her a quick hug. "How long has it been since your ma died, Katie?" she asked.

"It was last April," the little girl answered, a deep sadness touching her eyes as she remembered.

"You must miss her a lot," Sarah said, imagining how she would feel if Ma had died.

Katie nodded and swallowed hard. "I miss her something terrible!" she said. "She always smelled like lavender, and she smiled a lot. She was always singing as she worked around the house, cooking good food to eat and sewing pretty things. A lot like your ma, I reckon, except for the singing."

"My ma used to sing a lot when we lived in Miller's Forks," Sarah recalled. "Here, I reckon she's too tired, with so much work to do and not much to sing about."

Katie nodded. "It's hard to live out here. Back home, we had a little house at the end of the street, with a big garden in the back, and apple trees."

"We had apple trees, too," Sarah said. "And peach trees that bloomed pink in the springtime. And there was a barn with a hayloft where our cat always hid to have her kittens."

"I had a kitten once," Katie said sadly. "When the soldiers came, one of their horses stepped on it and killed it."

"How awful!" Sarah exclaimed. Her parents dead, her pet killed, she and her brother driven from their home—what other terrible things had this child endured? And at the hands of Patriots, for who else would hate Tories so?

All at once, Sarah knew that Tory or not, she would do anything she could to help this sad little girl find happiness.

Ruthie Larkin was waiting for Sarah and Jamie when they stopped for her on their way to school that morning. She had on her best blue dress, and her blond braids were tied with ribbons to match.

A light dusting of snow had fallen during the night, and Sarah thought, as she always did, that the hills looked like cakes with sugar frosting.

"You can sit with Jamie and share his paddle until Luke can make you one," Sarah said to Ruthie as they walked along together.

"All right, Sarah," Ruthie said agreeably, skipping a step in her excitement.

"'Miss Sarah,'" Jamie corrected. "At school, we have to call her 'Miss Sarah' because she's the teacher."

Ruthie frowned. "But I've always called her Sarah."

"Well, even I have to call her that, and I'm her brother," Jamie said.

"I want you to be the 'Keeper of Beauty' for our class, Ruthie," Sarah said quickly. "That means you can decorate the room with pretty leaves or whatever you want to make it look nice."

Ruthie nodded. "Ma says we're making hist'ry today, Sar . . . uh, Miss Sarah," she said. Then she added, "What's hist'ry?"

Sarah laughed. "Well, Ruthie, I reckon it means we're doing something that's never been done before. You are the first girl to go to school on Stoney Creek, and maybe in the whole Kentucky territory. In fact, I don't even know any girls who have gone to school in the state of Virginia! And I am the first teacher to have both boys and girls in her class."

Ruthie nodded again, but Sarah wondered if she had any idea what all that meant.

The morning passed uneventfully, with Ruthie fitting into the classroom routine as though she had always been there. Betsy already had taught her to recite her ABC's and to write her name, and she could count to ten.

At noon, when they had finished eating, Rob Willard asked if he could help David Mackey carry in wood. The stack of logs by the fireplace was nearly finished when both boys came running into the room, panting for breath, eyes wide with fright.

Fear clamped icy fingers around Sarah. "What is it, boys?" she cried. "What's wrong?"

"Miss Sarah," David panted, "There's tracks behind the woodpile. Big ones!" He held out both hands to show her how big.

"It's a painter, Miz Sarah!" Rob said. "I know it is! As big as a full-growed hog!"

"Hush, Rob!" Sarah warned as Ruthie began to cry, and little Caleb ran to grab his brother's pant leg with both hands.

"There's no panther that big, and you're scaring the children."

"Come here, Miz Sarah, and I'll show you," Rob insisted. "He's a big one, all right!"

Sarah let the boy take her hand and lead her to the door. Lying around the step was an armload of wood one of the boys had dropped in their haste to get back inside.

She peered cautiously around the yard, as she and Rob made their way to the woodpile. Out of the corner of her eye, she saw David and Caleb peering out the doorway, and the rest of the class apparently standing on a bench to look out the window.

Sarah gasped as Rob pointed to the animal tracks in the snow behind the woodpile. The tracks did appear to be those of some kind of cat, and whatever it was, it was very large.

That's all I need! Sarah thought. Already, she had an angry boy in the neighborhood who might want to get even with her for ordering him out of her classroom. Now, there was some kind of wildcat out there, perhaps waiting to pounce on one of them as they made their way home in the near dark. What could she do?

"I want to go home!" Ruthie wailed.

So do I! Sarah thought. But how could she get them all home safely? She didn't even have anything to fight off a wild animal. Should they just stay in the church building until some of the parents came to see what kept them?

"Lord, help me!" she whispered. "If You're ever going to direct my paths, as You promised in Proverbs 3: 5 and 6, do it now! Help me get these children home!"

She hurried Rob back inside the classroom and barred the door, trying desperately to think of a plan.

"Children, there does seem to have been a large wildcat

of some kind out in the yard last night or this morning," she explained honestly. "So we are going to go home right now, while it is good daylight, and we'll talk to our fathers about it so it will be safe to be here at school. Now, put away your paddles and pencils, gather your lunch bags, and come with me."

"Miss Sarah," David said, "cats don't like fire. Maybe if we carried burning pieces of wood it would stay away."

"You're right, David!" Sarah said, relief flooding through her. Why hadn't she remembered how Pa always kept a fire going on the trail to scare away wild animals?

"All right, children, we will go by twos. I want the oldest partner of each team to take a piece of kindling and light it in the fire. We will all walk home together. There's safety in numbers, you know. David, since you and Samuel and Caleb need to go in the opposite direction from the rest of us, we'll see you boys to your house first."

"That won't be necessary," a voice said, and Sarah looked up to see Trace Mackey's pale blue eyes peering in the window. "My brothers and I will walk you and the others to the Larkin cabin, where you can get Mark Larkin to see the rest of you home. Then the boys and I will go on home. We won't need the burning torches, because I have my gun." He held it up to show her.

Sarah had never been so glad to see anybody in her life! "Bank the fire, David," she said, first taking a burning stick from its edge. Then, as though nothing were unusual, she led her pupils out the door, pulled the latchstring through it, and motioned for them to follow Trace and his gun, two-by-two. She placed Ruthie and Jamie just slightly ahead of her, as she brought up the rear with her burning torch.

With every step she took, Sarah searched the trees above the path for the glowing yellow eyes that would tell her a cat crouched there, ready to pounce. But soon they were at the Larkins' place, and Ruthie ran inside to tell her family about the wildcat.

Luke came out, carrying his gun. "I'll see that this group gets home safely, Trace," he said.

Trace nodded, and turned to head on up the creek to the Mackey homestead.

Sarah reached out to stop him. "Thank you, Trace," she said. "You'll never know how glad I was to see you looking in the window with that gun in your hand!"

He looked at her solemnly, and if his pale eyes held mockery, she couldn't see it. "You're welcome," he mumbled. Then he led his brothers in the opposite direction, while she and Luke headed down the creek toward the Willard place, and then back home.

"I've seen some of those tracks out around the barn," Pa remarked when Jamie and Sarah told of their day's excitement. "He's a big one, all right. Right on one hundred pounds, unless I miss my guess. I wonder why he left the homesteads with livestock to wander down around the church? There's nothing for him there."

"Unless he wants religion," Luke said, laughing. "Or maybe he wants to learn his ABC's in Sarah's school!"

"That's not funny, Luke!" Ma scolded. "It just makes my blood run cold to think about those children alone in that isolated church being stalked by a cat!"

"I know the feeling!" Sarah agreed wholeheartedly.

"I'm thinking we need to close the school," Pa said.

"But Pa, we've only had five days!" Sarah protested. "They've just begun to learn! In three or four weeks, we can do a lot. I was planning a celebration before Christmas to invite everybody to see how much the children have learned."

"I'm sorry, Sary girl, but we can reopen your school in the spring, and you can have an Easter celebration."

"Oh, Pa, please!" she begged. "Can't you and the other men hunt down this wildcat and kill it? Or maybe the fathers and big brothers could take turns walking the children to school and picking them up in the evening."

"We couldn't take the time to guard the schoolhouse all day, Sary," he pointed out. "It isn't safe for you and those children to be outside without protection."

Sarah's hopes sank. She had been so happy with her little school, so proud of her position as teacher when she was only fourteen, so pleased with the eagerness of the children to learn. Now, it looked like her teaching career was over after only five days! By spring, the children might lose their enthusiasm. Their parents might lose their desire to have a school here on the banks of Stoney Creek.

Then she had an idea. "Pa, if we could find someone who would guard the children on the way to and from school and be there a couple of times each day when they had to be outside, we'd be perfectly safe inside the building with the door barred the rest of the time. Trace being there today with his gun made all the difference in the world!"

"I thought Trace made you nervous, staring at you with those icy eyes of his," Ma said.

"I was mighty glad to see those eyes peering in that schoolhouse window this afternoon, Ma!" she answered. "Pa, do you think someone would do it?"

"I'll bring it up after the meeting Sunday, and we'll see how the rest of the families feel about it," he promised.

"But Pa, couldn't we just try it for the rest of the week?" she begged.

He studied her for several seconds. "All right, Sary," he said finally. "I'll go talk to the other three families and see what they think. I suppose we could do it for one week. Crops are laid by, the winter's wood is cut. And maybe by next week we will have put an end to this cat."

He started out the door, then turned back. "But there's always dangers in the wilderness, Sary girl, and that church is at least a mile from any homestead. Before next spring, we might want to think about building a schoolhouse in sight of one of our cabins. The Indians will be back on the warpath then, and it will be planting season and time for the livestock to drop their young. We won't have time to spend our days guarding the schoolhouse."

"Whatever you say, Pa," Sarah agreed, knowing he was right, and knowing that, even if he weren't right, there was no use arguing with him. She was just glad he was going to try to keep the school open for now.

Sarah helped Ma get supper on the table, as Katie flitted around the cabin in her twice-handed-down dress, wearing her brooch that Ma had returned to her, waiting on Charlie hand and foot. She reminded Sarah of a little brown wren hovering over its only baby bird as she smoothed his covers and fluffed his pillow, took him a wet cloth to wash his face and hands, and ran to get him a fresh mug of water.

As they ate, Katie's eyes kept watching her brother's rapidly emptying plate. When he was down to half a biscuit, she jumped up to get him another one.

"Stop hovering over me, Katherine!" Charlie growled. "I feel like a doodlebug being prodded with a stick!"

At the hurt look on Katie's thin, pinched face, Sarah glared at the surly young man, but he didn't even notice.

"If you don't like the way she waits on you," Sarah snapped, "do it yourself!"

He looked up at her in surprise, then at Katie, who looked as if she might cry. "I'm sorry, Kate," he said. "You've done a good job of looking after me since I've been hurt."

Katie blushed with pleasure and ran to get him another mug of water.

Suddenly, Sarah had an idea. "How old are you, Katie?"

"I turned seven just after Ma died last April," she answered, sitting up as tall as she could.

"Can you read and write?"

"Ma taught me my letters," she mumbled, "but I can't read writing." She seemed to shrink into her oversized dress, as they all laughed.

Ma reached over and patted her hand. "We're not making fun of you, dear," she assured her.

"Not at all," Sarah said. "I was just wondering if you would like to go to school with us. I have one other little girl in the class, Ruthie Larkin, and I'd love to have you there."

Katie's smile started at her mouth and spread over her face until it lit her dark eyes. "Could I go, Charlie?" she begged.

Her brother stared moodily into the fire. "I'll think about it," was all he would promise.

14

To Sarah's surprise, the next morning Charlie grudgingly agreed to let Katie go with them to school.

The little girl ran around the cabin, torn between the excitement of getting ready for her first day of school and her uncertainty about leaving Charlie behind at the cabin.

"Katie, Ma will be here. He'll be perfectly all right," Sarah told her. "Hold still while I braid your hair."

Katie nodded. "I can't wait to learn how to read!" she said. "If I could have read the notice they tacked to that tree in our front yard, Charlie, I could have packed some things to bring with us. By the time you got home, it was too late, and there I was hiding in the hayloft with just my shawl and a few knickknacks of Ma's."

"It wasn't your fault, Kate," Charlie assured her with a half-smile a lot like hers. "The people there just didn't like Tories. They were determined to burn our house and run us out of town."

Sarah had heard many stories of how mean the Tories were to the Patriots. Now this boy was sitting here telling them that Patriots like her brother Nathan and her Uncle Ethan had treated his family very much like the Tories had treated Patriots in other places. Of course, she was sure neither Nate nor her uncle would do such things.

"It's hard to believe that people who were once neighbors could treat each other so cruelly, isn't it?" Ma asked. "Tories or Patriots—I suppose there's good and bad on both sides of this war." She got up from the table. "If you three are going to school, you'd best be on your way," she said then.

"You'd better wrap up good," Luke warned, coming in from the barn. "It's colder than blue blazes out there. The ground is frozen solid, and I had to break ice to get to the water in the spring this morning."

"I've got to make some warmer things for us to wear," Ma said, improvising cloaks for Jamie and Katie out of bed covers. "It's cold even inside the cabin this morning, and it looks like we are in for a long, hard winter."

Sarah helped the two little ones into shawls, scarves, and mittens, threw her own cloak around her shoulders, and tied a scarf over her ears.

"Let's go!" Luke said. "The quicker we leave, the quicker we can be inside the schoolhouse!"

"The quicker you can get back to Betsy's, you mean," Sarah teased, but he ignored her and left the cabin, carrying his gun.

"I know my letters and my numbers," Katie was babbling as they went out the door. "I just can't read letters all scrambled together on a page."

"Those are words, Katie," Sarah said. "I'll start teaching you how to figure them out today."

★ Chapter Fourteen ★

"Look! I made smoke!" Jamie called, as they hurried along, their footsteps leaving prints in the snow that still lay on the grass.

"It's just your warm breath hovering on the cold air," Sarah explained. "Wrap that scarf around your neck, Jamie. It's really cold!"

"That snow's hanging on for another one," Luke predicted, sounding just like Pa.

At the main trail, they met the Willard boys, escorted by their father, who scowled at Sarah, turned without a word, and headed back home.

The boys had thrust their hands into their buckskin shirts to keep warm, but their ears and necks under their coonskin caps were bare and red with cold.

"Pa says its foolish to have school in such weather," Will, Junior said, "but we didn't want to miss anything."

" 'Specially if that painter comes back!" Rob added.

"I'm not afraid of any old panther," Luke said. "I can hit him right between the eyes with one shot!"

"That's mighty big talk, brother!" Sarah said, but she knew it was true. She had heard Pa comment that Luke was one of the best marksmen in Kentucky.

"But I'd have to agree with your pa about the weather," Luke went on. "You'll never get that classroom warmed up today, Sarah!"

"If it stays this cold, Luke, I'll just give up and do what Pa says about closing school for the winter. I promise. I just wanted to go as long as we could."

Trace Mackey and his brothers were waiting for them at the Larkins', and little Ruthie came out with them, dressed in a bearskin coat and knitted scarf and mittens. She looked questioningly at Katie, and Sarah introduced their new classmate.

"Miss Sarah and I made hist'ry," Ruthie said proudly to Katie. "I forget how we did it. You can sit with Jamie and me," she said, taking Katie by the hand.

"I'll wait here at the Larkins for you, Sarah, and walk you all home this afternoon, but don't hold school too long. I want to get home before what little sun there is sets and it gets colder."

"Pa saw wildcat tracks around our barn, Trace," Sarah said as they walked on toward school. "I'm glad you're here with that gun."

"Yes, ma'am," he muttered, his eyes on the path ahead. "I . . . uh . . . guess I'll have to stay in the classroom today," he said then. "It's just too cold out here."

"Well, of course you will! I'm not that hardhearted!" Sarah responded with a laugh. "You can help teach the little ones," she added, as they entered the classroom.

She stole a glance at him and saw that his face was red. Was it just from the cold, or had she said something to embarrass him? Without a word, he took his usual seat at the back of the room, leaned back against the wall, and closed his eyes.

Sarah seated Katie beside Ruthie, and added the two new wooden paddles Luke had made to the stack on the front bench. Katie fit in with the class as smoothly as Ruthie had, and by the end of the day, she could write her name and Charlie's.

"Won't Charlie be surprised?" she asked Sarah happily as they headed home, Trace silently leading the way with his gun until they reached the Larkins where Luke took over.

The rest of the week didn't seem quite so cold on the trips to and from school, or inside the school, but the creek was still frozen solid, and Luke had been right about the snow. There was a new layer of white on top of the old.

★ Chapter Fourteen ★

Every one of Sarah's pupils was present every day, except little Caleb Mackey, who had come down with a bad cold. Sarah was glad they had continued to hold school, for by the end of the week, Katie was reading simple sentences, and could write all the letters of the alphabet.

Charlie, hobbling around the cabin now with the aid of a crutch Luke had cut him from a forked tree branch, praised the little girl and she beamed with joy.

Saturday, as soon as the noon meal was over, Ma said, "If you all will excuse me, I promised Rowena Larkin that Jamie and I would come visit a while this afternoon. I hate to traipse over there in the snow, but we want to get our quilt finished by the time the new Mackey baby makes his appearance into the world. Can you watch Elizabeth, Sarah, or do you want me to take her, too?"

"I'll keep an eye on her, Ma," Sarah said. "There's no need for you to tote her all the way over to the Larkins' place in this cold. Anyway, she's almost asleep in her plate! I'll put her down for a nap. Katie and I can work on her reading while you're gone."

Ma nodded, and reached for Jamie's hand. "We won't be gone long," she promised, leading the excited little boy out the door.

Sarah got up and stacked the dirty plates at one end of the table to make room for the dishwashing tub. She poured some cold water into the tub from the bucket, added hot water from the steaming teakettle over the fire, and shaved some lye soap into it.

"Ain't you afraid to stay here with me by yourself?" Charlie asked suddenly.

Sarah looked at him in surprise. "Why would I be afraid?"

"Well, you know I'm a desperate criminal, don't you?"

"So I've heard," she answered calmly, swishing her hand through the lye soap and water to make suds.

"Your pa was right to shoot me, I reckon," Charlie said then. "I know it's wrong to steal. But Katie and I were so hungry! We needed food."

Sarah turned to look straight into eyes as dark as Katie's. "Why didn't you just ask us for help, Charlie? Ma's never turned away anything sick or hungry in her life!"

"I don't know," he mumbled. "I . . . I didn't know what to do. People don't like Tories. And even though Pa was just a shopkeeper who had to charge taxes for the king, they blamed us all."

"That's not fair!" Sarah cried.

Katie nodded. "It was awful, Sarah! I was so scared!"

"I would have been scared, too, Katie!" Sarah said. "But it seems that God took care of you and Charlie."

Charlie snorted. "God had nothing to do with it! I took care of us, until your pa put that bullet through my leg. If there is such a thing as God, He hasn't been listening to any of our prayers!" he said bitterly.

"Charlie!" Katie gasped.

"I know how you feel, Charlie," Sarah said. "I blamed God for letting Pa take us away from home and bring us out here to the wilderness. I spent a miserable year in Kentucky feeling sorry for myself until I went back to Virginia and realized that I had only left the little house we had lived in there. Home was really my family, and I had taken it with me."

"But my family's dead, all except Kate here," Charlie pointed out. "If there is a God up there in heaven, he surely doesn't care what happens to us down here!"

"I don't believe that, Charlie," Sarah said firmly. "I used to think God was just some remote being way up there beyond the stars, but the Bible says God loved us so much that He sent his Son to the cross to take the punishment for our sins, so He surely cares what happens to us!"

"Yeah, Charlie," Katie chimed in, "that's what Ma used to tell us. Remember?"

"Ma was a woman," Charlie muttered. "Women always believe there's somebody up there who cares, who can make everything right. But the real world ain't like that, and it ain't always tied up in a pretty little package."

"Pa believed, too, Charlie," Katie insisted. "Don't you remember how he used to take all of us to that big white church in Charleston with the bells that rang from that tall steeple? Remember how Pa's voice would rumble out the words of the hymns? 'A mighty fortress is our God, a bulwark never failing!' " she sang in a mock bass voice.

Charlie snorted disdainfully.

"It's the devil who hates us and tries to do us harm, Charlie," Katie continued. "Remember the rest of that song? 'And still our ancient foe, would seek to work us woe . . . de dum de dum de dum' . . . I forget the rest," she finished.

"Then why does God allow the devil to do such awful things?" Charlie shot back. "If He's God, He could control the devil."

"I don't know, Charlie!" Katie wailed, suddenly bursting into tears. "I just know that Ma and Pa believed in God, and so do I! It's about all I've got left of our life together," she said sadly.

Sarah put an arm around Katie and pulled her close. "I don't understand why God allows Satan to do the things he does, Charlie," she said over the little girl's head. "I don't know why He didn't stop the soldiers from killing your pa or illness from taking your ma, but I believe He has kept you and Katie safe through it all."

Charlie snorted again. "I provided food and clothes for Kate and me. I found us dry places to sleep. I brought in wood for a fire. I can't think of anything any God off up there beyond the stars did to help us."

Sarah sighed. "Come to church with us tomorrow, Charlie. It'll just be mostly singing and praying. We don't have a regular preacher. But maybe God will send you some answers through somebody's testimony or something."

"Oh, Charlie, please!" Katie begged. "It's been so long since we've been to church! I admit I usually went to sleep during the long sermons, but I loved the singing! And I loved the time after the service when the grown-ups stood talking outside, and we played 'Devil on the Path,' and ran till—"

"I ain't going to no church service!" Charlie broke in, "and you ain't going, either, Katherine Louise! You will do as I say."

Sarah watched the hope die out of Katie's dark eyes and her little face fall into sadness once more.

"You're a cruel and selfish person, Charlie!" Sarah said. "You have no right to make your little sister suffer because you are all bitter and twisted up inside!"

A look of shame flitted across his face, followed by defiance. "I said we ain't going, and that's the end of it," he said. He picked up his forked stick and hobbled out the door.

Charlie didn't come back for supper that night, and Katie, convinced that he wouldn't come back at all, leaned against Sarah, sobbing quietly.

"Never you mind, Katie," Sarah comforted. "He'll come back when he remembers his warm pallet by the fire. And when he does, I'll get my pa after him. My pa knows God so well, you'd think he had breakfast with Him just this morning! If anybody can straighten out Charlie's thinking, it's Pa," she said, with much more confidence than she felt. She knew Pa would talk to him, but she wasn't sure Charlie would listen.

Katie, nevertheless, quietly cried herself to sleep. But after they had gone to bed, Sarah heard Charley hobble into the cabin and lie down on his pallet by the fireplace.

"All right, Mr. Charlie Whoever," she promised silently, "you will get the full treatment in the morning!"

Sarah waited until they all were seated around the table the next morning, Jamie and Elizabeth happily digging into plates of biscuits and gravy while Ma passed platters of bacon and eggs, before she brought up the subject.

"Pa, since God is all-powerful," she began, "why does He allow evil things to happen to good people?"

Pa studied the coffee in his cup for a moment. "That's a mighty big question, little girl," he said at last, his blue eyes meeting hers squarely across the table. "I've thought about it many times, and it seems to me that, like two countries at war have rules they cannot honorably break, God must have some kind of rules of honor in His battle with Satan. And God, being a gentleman, never breaks the rules."

Sarah glanced down the table to where Charlie sat buttering a biscuit. Was he listening?

"The Book of Job seems to bear this out," Pa continued. "When Satan asked God's permission to afflict Job, thinking that he would turn against his Maker when he began to suffer, God allowed him to test His servant, but He told Satan he could not take Job's life. He set the rules, and they both had to abide by them."

"But, Pa, Charlie's and Katie's ma and pa are dead," Sarah reminded him. "Why did God allow them to die?"

Pa took a deep breath, then a sip of coffee before he answered. "I don't think God sees death as a tragedy the way we do," he said, looking directly at Charlie. "When a person dies who has made his peace with God through the salvation offered by Jesus Christ, God welcomes him home with a happy celebration, just as the father welcomed home the prodigal son in the New Testament. I forget the chapter and verse."

"It seems to me, Hiram," Ma said, "that those answers are all well and good for the parents, but what about these children here who needed them. I guess I don't quite understand it either."

"Well, Della, you have to realize that I'm not God, and I can't answer for Him, outside of what He has told us in His Word. Some things we just have to accept on faith, knowing He has said, 'All things work together for good to those who love God.' And that's found in Romans 8:28," he added.

Pa's answers made sense to Sarah, though she didn't quite understand all that he had said. She needed time to think about it, to study the Scriptures he had named. She glanced again at Charlie, who sat staring at his plate, as though it was there he would find his answers to what troubled him.

"We had best finish our breakfast and get ready for church," Pa said then. "By the way, our young preacher is still here. I saw him yesterday when I went over to help the Strausbergs kill hogs. He was there helping, too."

Sarah held her breath, but Pa was off on another topic. "We'll be killing two of our hogs next week, Della," he said. "Mr. Strausberg says they will help and we can borry their sausage mill."

"Is he going to preach today, Pa?" Sarah asked.

"Mr. Strausberg? I don't think so," Pa said, with a twinkle in his Irish-blue eyes. "But I suspect Brother Justice may give it another try."

He looked at Charlie. "Do you want me to hitch up a horse so you can ride to church?" he asked. "It's only a couple of miles, but I don't think you should try to walk it on that bum leg."

"No, sir. I don't plan to go," Charlie answered politely, but with a stubborn look on his face. "And I don't aim for Kate to go, either."

Pa studied him for several seconds. "All right. I reckon

you're the man of your household, and I won't interfere with that. But remember what the Lord Jesus Himself said about those who hinder the little children to come unto Him. Don't end up with a millstone around your neck, young man."

"You'll be missing a good sermon," Ma coaxed, leading Jamie over to the bed to get him ready.

Sarah hurried into the next room to dress Elizabeth and herself. She could hardly wait to hear what the preacher would have to say today. He was so interesting, not all dry and dusty like most of the preachers she had heard.

What should she wear? The dress she had worn to the Governor's Ball last Christmas was too fancy to wear to church in the wilderness, she decided. Anyway, it might remind the preacher of how rude she had been the last time she had seen him. She reckoned she'd just have to wear the Sunday blue silk again her Aunt Charity had made for her to wear to church in Williamsburg.

Soon they were all ready to go, except for Charlie, who sat on his pallet staring into the fire, and little Katie, who was trying her best to pretend she didn't want to go.

Sarah gave the little girl a quick hug and followed her family out the door and up the creek bank toward the church, wishing Charlie had come along, or at least let Katie attend worship service with them.

As she took her seat beside Ma, Sarah saw the preacher was already inside the building. She supposed he had come with the Strausbergs, who came early to build the fire each Sunday in cold weather.

"I didn't expect to be back here so soon," Jeremy Justice said, when the singing was finished and he was called to the front to speak. "But I've enjoyed my week with the Strausbergs, even if Papa Strausberg has done his level best to work me to death, and Mama Strausberg has done her level best to founder me with wonderful food!"

As the congregation laughed, Sarah found herself impatient for the preacher to get on with his sermon. What strange and wonderful things would he have to relate to them today?

"I will be moving on tomorrow morning," he said. "My next preaching engagement is several day's walk from here. But, if you want me, I can come back three Sundays after that."

After the Amens had died away, he said seriously, "Folks, my life has changed greatly since I accepted God's call on that battlefield. Some of you responded to the call of the Lord last Sunday, and there should be some changes in your life. But those who have not answered the call of God have this to look forward to."

Then, with great dramatic flair, he launched into a portrayal of someone just arriving in hell with such persuasive skill that Sarah felt cold chills travel down her spine. She could feel the searing heat, hear the awful screams. She was suffocating in the thick and terrible darkness of separation from God. There was no light. There was no hope.

There was a thud behind her, and Sarah turned to see that Mrs. Mackey had fainted and fallen between the benches. Caleb Mackey began to cry, followed by Ruthie, Jamie, and Elizabeth. Sarah saw that the two other Mackey boys had edged over closer to their father, and the Willard boys were holding hands tightly.

The preacher stopped in mid-sentence. "Some of you ladies please tend to our fallen one. I apologize for making the story so graphic, but folks, I am compelled to do everything in my power to keep everyone I can from going to that terrible place."

Sarah looked back and saw that Mrs. Mackey was back on her bench, being fanned vigorously by Mrs. Larkin and Mrs. Strausberg.

"I believe that God is a God of love," Jeremy Justice went on, "for John 3:16 tells us that 'God so loved the world that He sent his only begotten Son that whosoever believeth in him should not perish but have everlasting life.' What greater love can there be than that? And, as a God of love, He sends no one to spend eternity in such a horrible place, but we send ourselves there by our refusal to accept the salvation He has so lovingly provided. I repeat what I asked you last Sunday: How can we escape if we neglect so great a salvation?"

This time, it was the Willards who beat everybody to the front of the building to fall on their knees in repentance, even Rachel. But Sarah couldn't help thinking that Rachel was very conscious of how pretty she looked with her full skirts spread out gracefully around her and just enough tears to brighten her green eyes as she looked up beseechingly at the preacher.

"Shame on you, Sarah Moore!" she scolded herself silently. "You have no right to judge, when you yourself are only escaping from the flames of hell by the grace of God!"

All the way home, Sarah's thoughts were on the preacher and the strange message he had preached. She wished Charlie had been there to hear it. There was no way she could make him feel what she had felt as Jeremy Justice spoke about hell, but she would do her best to relate all that she had heard. Maybe Charlie would go next time.

Charlie had already gone, though, but not to church. He had taken Katie and gone back to the pitiful life they had known before Sarah had discovered them in the cave. Sarah knew it the minute she walked into the cabin. His pallet was rolled up neatly by the fireplace. The meat and biscuits left over from breakfast were gone, along with what potatoes had been in the basket in the corner and a string of beans from the wall.

On the table, again, lay Katie's gold brooch, its jewels sparkling in the sunlight that fell through the open door.

"That poor child!" Ma exclaimed. "She wants so badly to do right, but she loves her brother."

Sarah blinked away tears. Already, she had become attached to the little girl. She had wanted to teach her to read, to help her deal with the loss of her mother, to make the sad little face light up more often with one of those rare smiles.

"That confounded boy has run off with one of my horses!" Pa said angrily as he came into the cabin. "I knew something was amiss when I saw the barn door ajar."

"He's taken Katie with him," Sarah said, "and some provisions. See? They left the brooch again to pay for them."

"He has a right to take his little sister with him, and I don't begrudge them some of our food. But that scalawag has no right to half of my team of horses!" Pa stormed.

"I reckon he felt he couldn't get far on that half-healed leg," Ma tried to excuse the boy.

"Then he should have stayed until he was well," Pa said. "I'm going after that young man right now, and he'd better hope I don't catch him!"

Before Pa could leave, though, Luke came bursting through the doorway, panting for breath.

"There's Indian signs down by the river!" he said.

16

Appears to be a sizable party of Indians crossed the river just above the Willard place," Luke said. "Mr. Mackey has sent Trace to warn the Strausbergs and the preacher. They're trying to decide if they should all hole up in one cabin, or stay at home and protect their own homesteads. I tried to get Betsy's family to come over here, but they wouldn't leave."

"What about the Willards?" Pa asked, Charlie and his stolen horse seemingly forgotten.

"I'm on my way to warn them now," Luke said. "Pa, is it all right if I ride Willie?"

Pa's face flushed angrily again. "That Charlie has run off with Willie," he said. "Just when we most need two horses! If I ever get my hands on that boy . . ."

"Now, Hiram," Ma put in, "calm down. They did leave the brooch to pay for everything."

"I can't ride a brooch!" Pa shouted. "By the time I could sell it and buy another horse, our scalps would all be dangling from some brave's belt!"

He walked over to the window and slid the bar across the shutter. "Luke, ride Bess over to the Willards," he said then, "and invite them to join us here. If the Indians crossed above their place, they could be headed there, or they may have taken to the woods and be headed here. If the Willards don't want to leave their place, let them be and hurry back. As soon as this Indian scare is over, I'm going after that thieving Charlie!"

Ma called, "Be careful, son!" as Luke ran out the door.

Pa barred the other windows. He handed Sarah the water buckets and picked up both the small and the large iron kettle.

"Come to the spring with me, Sary, and help me lay us in a supply of water just in case we can't get to the spring for a while, or in case a flaming arrow should set the cabin afire," he explained.

When they had filled every available container with water and placed them safely inside the cabin, Pa sent Sarah to the storage hole to bring in some cabbages, potatoes, and onions, while he went to the shed after a supply of meat.

"That thieving rascal has taken our last side of bacon!" he reported when he came back.

Ma looked at the ham and the smoked venison he carried. "Are you expecting a siege, Hiram?" she asked, stirring something she had cooking in the iron spider as though it were an everyday thing to expect Indians to ride into the yard at any moment.

"With Indians, you just never know what to expect," Pa answered, dropping a load of firewood beside the fireplace. "It's late in the year for an Indian raid, as it is. And unless the siege is of very short duration, we can't . . ." He stopped. "Anyway, it's always better to be safe than sorry."

★ Chapter Sixteen ★

"Wouldn't it be safer for all the families on Stoney Creek to try to fight off the Indians in one place?" Ma asked.

"We'd have a better chance if we all were together, but then all the empty homesteads would be burned. Still, we might save our lives, and that's the most important thing," Pa said.

"Which place would be the easiest to defend?" Sarah asked.

"We've got the only two-story cabin, Sary," Pa answered. "It's always easier to fire down upon attackers from the second story. Visibility is better, and the Indians have a harder time trying to climb up on the roof to set it afire or to slip down the chimney. I built this cabin with safety in mind. But then none

of the others want to leave their homesteads unprotected, I'm sure. We'll just stay here, and if some of the others come to join us, we'll make them welcome."

In a few minutes, Luke was back. "The Willards don't want to leave their place," he reported, "though I think Rachel would have come home with me in a heartbeat," he added with a grin.

"Luke!" Ma scolded.

"Rachel, is it?" Sarah said. "Shame on you, Luke! And you engaged to be married in just a few months!"

"Hey, I didn't say I wanted her to come home with me," he protested. "I just said I thought she would have. She was flashing those green eyes at me like she always does at church."

"Like she does at everything in breeches!" Sarah corrected.

Pa threw the heavy wooden bar across the door. "Well, you may have to fight off more than some feisty little gal, son," he said sarcastically. "Come help me get our am-munition ready."

"I dare any Indian to try to burn this place after all the work we put into rebuilding it!" Luke was saying, as he followed Pa up the stairs.

"Ma, you're so calm!" Sarah marveled. "Aren't you afraid?"

"Well, Sarah, I've known this day would come sooner or later. There's nothing we can do but pray, try to keep our wits about us, and do whatever we can to survive."

"What can I do to help?" Sarah asked.

"Keep the children occupied," Ma said, still stirring her cooking. "I don't want them scared until they have to be."

Jamie raced around the cabin with his stick gun. "Bang! Bang!" he yelled. "Take that, you Indian!"

"Settle down, Jamie," Sarah ordered, "before you get Elizabeth all upset."

Elizabeth looked up from under her cornsilk bangs, an innocent smile on her sweet little face that lit up her pretty blue eyes. She toddled over and held out her hands for Sarah to lift her up into her arms.

Suddenly, Sarah's heart wrenched. *What if the Indians came and Pa and Luke were not able to hold them off? What if they killed all of them, or took Elizabeth and Jamie captive, as they often did the settlers' children?*

She pushed the thoughts away, and bent down to pick up Elizabeth. *There's no need to borrow trouble,* she thought, carrying the baby into the other room to put her down for a nap. Then she wondered if it would be safer to put her upstairs in Luke's bed.

A knock sounded at the door, and Sarah's heart stopped, then started with a thump as she heard a voice with a heavy German accent call out, "It's us! The Strausbergs! We've come for shelter!"

Ma hurried to the door and drew back the bar. "Come in," she invited. "You're more than welcome! The more the merrier when you're under siege!" she said, as though inviting them in for a party.

"Then I don't suppose you'll mind my crowding in, too," Sarah heard a deep voice say. Automatically, her face flushed bright red. The preacher was out there! How long could she stall here in the bedroom getting Elizabeth to sleep? she wondered, as she heard Ma slide the bar back in place across the door. How long before she had to go into the other room and greet their guests?

All at once, Sarah noticed an unnatural stillness around the cabin. No birds chattered in the cornfield on their way south for the winter. No chickens clucked, no ducks gabbled in the yard. There was no sound from the cows or their one remaining horse. Then, deep in his throat, she heard Hunter growl.

Suddenly, a terrible screeching began outside the cabin, and Pa's and Luke's guns went off upstairs. She heard footsteps taking the stairs at a run.

"I know we must defend ourselves," she heard the preacher's voice say from up in Luke's room, "but I hate killing these poor heathen souls before I have a chance to try to lead them to God. Christ died for them, too, you know."

"I know how you feel, but it's hard to lead a man to God when he's waving his tomahawk over your head," Sarah heard Pa answer. Luke laughed. Then the guns went off again, three of them this time.

"Mama, I go upstairs now to help vit shooting Indians. You vill be all right?" Sarah heard Mr. Strausberg say.

"Of course, Papa! Fight them off goot or ve all vill be dead!" his wife answered.

Then the clamor was so great Sarah was reminded of the siege she had endured with the settlers at Harrodstown, when Indians had surrounded the fort for days, coming out of the forest again and again, screeching and yelling and shooting flaming arrows. Only this time, there were only her pa and Luke, one old German, and a preacher to fight them off. She prayed there were fewer Indians out there to fight!

Then she heard Pa call, "Della, you all come up here where it's safer. And Sary, we need you to load for us!"

Sarah scooped up Elizabeth and carried her up the stairs, followed by Mrs. Strausberg and Ma, leading Jamie. She laid the baby on Luke's bed and took her place under the window beside Pa and the preacher. Luke and Mr. Strausberg were stationed at the window facing the barn.

"There's not more than a dozen of them out there, and they're not wearing war paint," Pa said as he handed Sarah his extra gun to load. "It's late in the year for them to be out hunting, but it's most likely a hunting party looking for some fun on their way home. We may be able to hold them off, unless more join them."

Sarah knew from the long, weary hours she had spent

loading Pa's and Luke's guns at the fort during the Indian siege, that there should be one loader for each shooter. But since they had only this one extra gun, she would load it and then reload the first empty one.

"Do you think other parties have gone to the other homesteads?" the preacher asked.

"Ve maybe don't haf a homestead by now!" Mr. Strausberg said sadly, taking deadly aim.

"It's all right, Papa," Mrs. Strausberg assured him. "If ve survive, ve can rebuild."

"That's the old pioneer spirit!" Luke said.

The preacher turned and took the loaded gun from Sarah, then handed her his empty one. He smiled at her, and she smiled back, hoping her blush came after he had turned back to the window.

A flaming arrow flew through the open window and lodged in a log of the wall behind them. Ma grabbed it and smothered the fire with her skirt. Another landed on the floor, and Mrs. Strausberg stamped it out with her foot.

"Jamie, take Elizabeth under the bed with you," Ma ordered, and the little boy did as he was told without question, but Sarah heard a whimper from under the bed.

"Teach Elizabeth to play mousie, Jamie," she reminded him. "Remember how we played mousie when the Indians came before?" She doubted if he did, for he had been about Elizabeth's size when the Indians had attacked Ma that day.

"Shhhh, 'Lizbeth!" she heard him say. "Play like we're little mousies hiding in our hole!" *He did remember,* Sarah thought gratefully, noting that Elizabeth had grown quiet.

Two more arrows whizzed through the window, but these were not on fire. Then there was a loud whoop from outside.

"Are they leaving?" the preacher asked. "Look, they're

gathering up their fallen!"

Luke shouted, "The rascals are setting the barn on fire!"

Then there was silence. Sarah raised up to look out the window just in time to see the remaining Indians riding into the woods behind the barn, each of them leading at least one horse carrying the body of another Indian.

17

Sarah stood at the upstairs window, watching the men work feverishly at the barn to put out the fire the Indians had set. Except for a few smoldering spots on the roof that Luke and the preacher were dousing with water, and a wisp of smoke here and there, the barn soon seemed secure. Pa and Mr. Strausberg, though, were tethering the frightened livestock to the fence, away from the smell of smoke and fire.

Suddenly, Sarah realized that the Indians had ridden off in the direction of the cave where she had discovered Katie and Charlie. Had they gone back there to hide when they left the cabin this morning? Would the Indians find them there, defenseless?

"Ve had best be getting home now, if ve still got a home," Sarah heard Mrs. Strausberg say to Ma.

"Why don't you let the men ride over to your place and see that everything is all right, and we can fix supper for them here," Ma suggested. "It's not that far away."

That meant the preacher would be here for the evening meal, Sarah thought in dismay. *What could she find to say to him?* But after spending the afternoon with him fighting off Indians, why should she feel embarrassed around him anymore?

She looked around for Jamie and Elizabeth, and found both of them sound asleep under Luke's bed. Rather than disturb them, she left them there to finish their naps and went downstairs.

Ma had Mrs. Strausberg slicing cabbage and potatoes into the small kettle, while she prepared to roast a chunk of venison over the fire.

"Sarah, you gather the eggs, then come back and straighten up the cabin a bit," Ma said. "We're having company for supper."

"Ma, those Indians rode off in the direction Katie and Charlie probably took this morning. If they come upon them . . ."

Ma's eyes widened and her hands flew to cover her mouth. "Oh, Sarah!" she said. "I was so happy to see the Indians leaving, I never once thought about Katie and Charlie."

"The yard's clear of Indians, Della," Pa announced coming into the cabin with Luke and the preacher close behind him. "Now, what's this about Charlie? I'm going to find that rapscallion if it's the last thing I do!" he vowed.

"Charlie?" Mr. Strausberg questioned. "Who is this Charlie?"

"He's one of the thieves that have plagued us these past weeks," Pa explained. "My wife nursed him back to health from a bullet wound I put in his leg. We took care of them here for over a week. Then, while we were at church this morning, the ungrateful wretches left with half of my team of horses!"

"So that's who vas stealing from us?" Mr. Strausberg said.

Pa nodded. "A half-grown boy and his sister. We had not yet decided what to do with them."

"They were just children, really," Ma added, "orphans taking what they needed to survive in the wilderness."

"Orphans?" Mrs. Strausberg echoed. "Poor little kinder!"

"Pa, the Indians rode off in the direction of that cave where we found Charlie and Katie," Sarah interrupted. "Do you suppose they might have gone back there? If the Indians find them, you know they'll kill them!"

"We are going to ride around to the other homesteads to see what damage, if any, has been done," Pa said. "On our way back, we will ride over by the cave."

"But, Pa, that may be too late!"

"Sary," Pa said, "if the Indians left that way and found Charlie and Katie in that cave, it is already too late."

Sarah bit her lip, trying not to cry right there in front of the Strausbergs and the preacher. She couldn't bear to think of little Katie in the clutches of those wild-looking braves! Or Charlie, either, for that matter. But when Pa set his head, there was nothing she could do about it, she thought, watching the four men leave the cabin.

At the doorway, the preacher turned. "You were a great help this afternoon, Sarah. Thank you," he said with one of those smiles that for some strange reason seemed to melt her insides and set her face afire.

"You're welcome," she mumbled, turning away as though she had something important to do over by the fireplace. She didn't look back until she heard the door shut behind him.

"I think our Sarah has a yearning to be a preacher's vife," Mrs. Strausberg teased.

"Mrs. Strausberg! I have no such thing!" Sarah said indignantly.

Ma smiled. "He's a nice young man," was all she said.

"Ya, he is that," Mrs. Strausberg agreed. "A smidgen strange, but nice."

Sarah grabbed her cloak and left the cabin before Ma could tell her she couldn't go. She'd rather face Indians than stay in the cabin and be teased about the preacher, she decided. What was it about that preacher, anyway? He hadn't affected her this way when he was a clerk at Greenhow's Store or a militiaman in Williamsburg. She was acting as silly as her cousin Tabitha over Seth Coler or Abigail over the dancing master. And she had made such fun of them!

Sarah walked to the barn and saw that there was little real damage from the Indians' fire. All the animals seemed to be unharmed, too.

What about Katie and Charlie, though? She looked off behind the barn into the trees. Suddenly, Sarah had to know what had happened to them, so she set off toward the cave. Pa and Ma would have a fit if they knew she was out in the woods alone. Who knew where those Indians were! In fact, she wasn't too happy about it herself! Still, her need to know pushed her onward.

At the pine thicket, she stopped and sniffed the air, but with the smoke from the burning barn still hovering over the valley below, it was hard to tell if there was a campfire nearby. She eased over to where she could see the opening to the cave in the rocks. It was there, dark and unwilling to share its secrets.

Sarah took a deep breath and left the cover of the thicket to climb toward the opening. Cautiously, she peered inside, but the cave was as empty as Jesus' tomb on Easter morning. There was no sign that Katie and her brother had been there today.

★ Chapter Seventeen ★

Suddenly, Sarah heard the ring of a horseshoe against stone, and her heart began to pound against her ribs. She looked around wildly, then slipped inside the cave to hide. The Indians must be back! But Indians didn't shoe their horses, did they?

Hope sprang up inside her. Maybe it was Charlie and Katie, riding on Willie, coming back to the cave!

She peered around the opening of the cave and saw a horse come around the hillside toward her. It *was* Willie! But there was no one on his broad back. His reins dangled loosely around his neck.

A sob tore through her. The Indians must have captured Katie and Charlie. Either their scalps already had been added to some brave's collection, or they were well on their way to the Indians' winter camp to become slaves. It was the only explanation for finding this riderless horse wandering along the hillside, and she didn't think she could bear it!

"Willie!" she called softly. "Whoa, there!" She scrambled down the rocks and grabbed the horse by his mane. She wound her fingers through the long, coarse hair, climbed up on a rock, and pulled herself up on his back. She nudged him in the sides with her heels, and Willie trotted obediently along down the hill, heading for his barn and supper.

"Dear God," Sarah prayed as she rode, "please don't let Katie and Charlie suffer. They've been through so much already! Please, if they're still alive, take care of them, and, if it's Your will, bring them back to us someday." She closed the prayer, but every few feet, she found herself praying the same prayer all over again.

Sarah rode into the barn lot, slid off Willie's back, and put him in the barn with the other animals Pa had returned to their stalls. She gave him some hay and several ears of corn. Then she went to the cabin to tell Pa she had found his horse, and to tell Ma what she suspected had happened to Katie and Charlie.

Pa jumped up and ran to the barn to make sure his horse was all right.

Ma dabbed at her eyes with her apron, then began to tell Mrs. Strausberg all about her former patient and his little sister.

"I never had the babies to raise," Mrs. Strausberg said sadly. "I buried three, all dead vhen they came into this vorld, vit never a chance to live."

"I'm so sorry, Mrs. Strausberg," Ma said, patting the older woman's shoulder. "I buried one, our firstborn, a girl. She only lived seven hours. I reckon that's why Sarah has always been so precious to me. And now the good Lord has blessed us with little Elizabeth."

Sarah looked at Ma in amazement. She had never heard that!

"The goot Lord dit not see fit to bless us vit any," Mrs. Strausberg said. "But I am sure He knows best." She sighed. "Maybe ve vould not make goot parents, after all."

"I don't believe that!" Ma exclaimed. "You would make very good parents, I am sure, and wonderful grandparents. You remind me of my own grandparents on my mother's side. They were wonderful people, and I spent every possible moment with them, until our pa moved us to Virginia."

Again, Sarah looked at her in surprise. She recalled stories Ma had told her about these grandparents, and that they had lived in Connecticut before they came to Miller's Forks. It had not dawned on her, though, that Ma had gone through the same uprooting she had when Pa moved them to Kentucky.

The door opened, and Luke and the preacher came into the cabin.

★ Chapter Seventeen ★

"That young Rachel Willard is just like you said she was, Luke," the preacher said. "I wasn't sure I'd get out of there with my reputation intact!"

"You'll be wise to be on the lookout for little Rachel," Luke agreed. "I'd be scared to death to live in the same neighborhood with her if I didn't have the protection of my coming marriage to my sweet Betsy!"

"By the way, I'll be glad to do the honors, any time you say," the preacher said seriously, slapping Luke on the back. Then he turned to the rest of them. "The Indians stopped here first, for some reason. All the other homesteads are unharmed, I'm happy to report."

Mrs. Strausberg grabbed the preacher and gave him a big hug. Then she kissed him on both cheeks.

"Oh, oh!" Luke said. "There goes your reputation, after all!"

The preacher gave Mrs. Strausberg a hug in return. "Oh, well," he sighed, "if I've learned anything in my twenty years on this earth, it's that character is what counts, not reputation!"

Sarah busied herself with setting the table. Then she helped Ma dish up supper. Finally, she had run out of excuses, and she had to sit down to eat with the rest of them.

When she looked up, she found that by chance or by someone's design, she was seated right across the table from Jeremy Justice.

Sarah kept her eyes on her plate, only looking up to pass food, and then never directly across the table. She could feel the preacher's eyes upon her, though, from time to time.

"This has been a day I won't soon forget," he said finally, as he ladled a second helping of cabbage and potatoes onto his plate. "The response to my message this morning was gratifying. My afternoon was interesting, to say the least! And I have had a delicious supper surrounded by good friends."

Sarah could feel his eyes upon her, but she concentrated on buttering a piece of cornbread as though her life depended on getting it just right. If Luke were there, she knew he would have had something to say about the preacher meeting Rachel Willard, too, but Luke had gone back over to have supper with Betsy and the Larkins.

"We've been glad to have you with us," Ma said, refilling Jamie's plate with meat and vegetables. "We were especially thankful to have you here while those Indians were racing around out there, threatening our lives!"

"I've fought many battles against the redcoated army of the British, but this was my first taste of Indian warfare," the preacher admitted. "I hope it will be my last. I'd much rather win their souls than kill them. But I have to agree with you, Mr. Moore, that it is very difficult to preach to someone who is waving a tomahawk over your head or trying his best to shoot an arrow into you!"

Pa laughed. "We appreciate you coming here to hold services for us," he said then. "Is there any way we could persuade you to stay and be our preacher?"

"Ya, ve vould like that," Mr. Strausberg agreed. "Ve need a preacher out here in the vilderness to keep us civilized."

Sarah held her breath, not knowing whether she wanted this Jeremy Justice to say he would be their preacher, or if she would prefer never to see him again.

"In my travels around to the Kentucky settlements, I have felt that my messages were particularly effective in four of them," he answered slowly. "I have been thinking that I might offer to preach in each of them once a month, reserving that fifth Sunday that comes every three months or so to hold a service in some new settlement."

"And is the Stoney Creek church one of these four?" Pa asked.

The preacher smiled. "Yes, it is. I think I might even look around here for some land where I could build a cabin and maybe open a small store. I would want to support myself and not be a burden on my congregations. I have experience with merchandising, you know. It was while I was a clerk in John Greenhow's Store in Williamsburg, in fact, that I first met Sarah."

★ Chapter Eighteen ★

Startled that he remembered that first encounter when she had gone to the store to buy raisins for Aunt Charity and had been embarrassed because she had not known how to order them, Sarah looked up, directly into his smiling blue eyes.

"I had never seen green eyes like yours, Sarah," he said. "The dress you wore at the Governor's Ball was exactly the same color. Do you still have it?"

She nodded, feeling that awful telltale blush creep over her face. "Rachel Willard has green eyes," she said defensively.

"Yes, she does," he agreed, "the color of grass, and they flash and dance. But yours have a depth and a stillness, like looking into a deep, green pool of creek water where you can't see the bottom."

Sarah wished the floor would open up and swallow her. She didn't know where to look. Certainly not at him! And not at her family or their guests, who had heard all that!

"You know, you can tell a lot about a person by his eyes," he went on. "Yours, Mr. Moore, are the smoky blue of the Irish and have more than a hint of Gaelic mischief in them. Your brown eyes, Mr. Strausberg, look the world straight in the face without flinching. Yours, Mrs. Strausberg, have been hardened by the tragedies you have witnessed, but underneath, there is a soft gentleness."

"You are very perceptive, young man," Mrs. Strausberg said. "It is because of de kinder I buried, I tink."

Suddenly, Sarah wondered if he remembered that rainy night when, as a Patriot militiaman patrolling the streets of Williamsburg, he had found her trying to make her way home from an encounter with her tutor, Gabrielle, and her friend, the infamous British spy known as the Demon Devon.

He had escorted her safely home, warning her not to go out again because a dangerous British spy was on the loose. She hoped he didn't remember, or that he was still unaware of her misguided involvement with their enemies! She could feel the blush deepening, this time with shame.

"Is there anything we can do about the missing children?" she heard the preacher ask then.

"We rode by the cave this afternoon and found nothing, not even a hint that anybody had been there. We found no Indian signs after they left the road Luke and I cut for hauling wood," Pa answered. "But would you gentlemen be willing to ride into the forest at daybreak with me to try again to pick up the trail, either of the Indians or of the children?"

Jeremy Justice nodded. "Even if we are too late to rescue them, maybe we can at least discover what happened to them."

"I vill go," Mr. Strausberg said.

Daybreak? Sarah thought. The Indians might travel all night, taking their captives far beyond the Ohio River into unknown Indian territory where they would never be heard from again. But she knew there was little hope of picking up the trail at night in the dark forest. What could she expect Pa to do? Still, it just seemed that there ought to be something!

Memories of little Katie haunted Sarah. She was such a sad little thing, and so eager to learn! And she had reminded her so much of Meggie that she had grown attached to her in no time. If only there was something she could do! But, even if Katie were still alive, what could she do to rescue her, one fourteen-year-old girl against five savages?

She wished their Indian friend, the Little Captain, were here. He had helped her save her friend Marcus's son, as well as his wife, Dulcie, and the Reynolds' slave, Malinda, from the Indians. He would know what to do to find Katie and Charlie, if they were still alive. But the last she had heard of the Little

Captain, he had gone on another errand for his hero, "General S'washington," proudly wearing his blue Patriot soldier's coat with its one remaining brass button. There was no telling where he was right now.

"If you find the kinder," Sarah heard Mrs. Strausberg say, "ve vould be glad to gif them a home. It vould be a blessing to us to haf them. Maybe that is why the goot Lord never allowed our babies to live. Maybe He wanted us to give a home to someone else's orphan kinder."

"You may be right, Mama!" her husband exclaimed. "I haf never thought of it that vay."

"Please don't get your hopes up, Mrs. Strausberg," Pa cautioned. "It is very unlikely that we will find them. They are most likely dead at the hands of the Indians, or well on their way to some hidden Indian village far beyond the Ohio River."

As she helped clean up after supper, the hopelessness of Pa's words sank deep into Sarah's heart. As she dressed Elizabeth in her nightgown and put her to bed, the image of little Katie climbing into the trundle bed beside them in Jamie's nightshirt brought a lump to her throat. She lay down on the bed beside Elizabeth and quietly cried herself to sleep.

Pa's scouting party rode out at sunrise, long before Sarah and Jamie left for school.

All morning, as she helped Ruthie write her letters and Samuel begin to figure out words, Sarah thought about Katie and how much the little girl had loved being in school. Where was she now? What was she doing? Was she still alive?

Unwilling to dwell on that, Sarah let her gaze roam around the room and fall on Trace, sitting at the back with his eyes closed. She couldn't tell if he were asleep or just bored.

She was glad he was there with his gun to guard them, but she was sorry he had to sit cooped up there all day, listening to the children repeat things he must have known for years.

After lunch she asked, "Would you like to read the children their Bible story today, Trace?" She always read to them while they rested.

Trace sat up straight and looked at her. Then he looked down at the floor. He shifted his feet. "Naw," he said finally. "I think I'll go out and . . . uh . . . scout around some." He picked up his gun and left the room.

He came back into the building just before time to go home, and motioned for her to come to the back of the room.

"He's still around," he said in a voice the children could not overhear. "There's cat tracks around the woodpile again, and I saw some up by the trail, too."

"Do you think we can get the children home safely?"

"I reckon that's what I'm here for," he said, a smirk of a smile touching his lips. "But if David's going to get in his wood, I need to go with him."

She nodded. "David," she said, "Trace is going to guard you while you bring in your wood, so make it quick. The wildcat has been back, and we need to get home."

Other than tracks, though, they saw nothing of the wildcat, and made it to the Larkins', picked up Luke, and got home well before dark.

Pa was just coming through the gate. Sarah's heart sank at the solemn look on his face. He shook his head at her, and she braced herself for what he might say.

"We picked up the Indians' trail about halfway up the hill," he said. "Then they turned toward the river. They crossed the Kentucky and headed north, aiming for the Ohio territory, or I miss my guess."

"But what about Katie and Charlie?" Sarah asked, afraid that any news of them would be bad news.

★ Chapter Eighteen ★

Pa shook his head again. "If the Indians got 'em, they didn't leave a sign," he said. "Of course, the good news is, we didn't find their mutilated bodies along the trail, either, so there's a chance they may still be alive."

"Hiram, do you think they might have made it to one of the forts?" Ma asked hopefully.

Sarah looked at him eagerly, but he only shrugged his shoulders. "Your guess is as good as mine, Della. Our preacher went on over toward Logan's Fort and Harrodstown. He'll let us know what he finds out when he comes back next month."

Next month? Sarah thought in dismay. "You're not going to trail the Indians any farther?" she asked. "Just in case."

"Sary, if there was any indication that they had those children, we'd follow those rascals all the way to their village. But I'm not going to ask the men of this neighborhood to leave their homes and families unprotected while we go chasing after some 'might be,'"he answered. "I just feel that, if those Indians had them, we would have picked up some sign—some hair on a bush, a scrap of cloth, something."

"Indians are clever, Hiram. They can come and go like shadows, and no one even knows they're around," Ma said.

"That thieving Charlie's clever, too," Pa answered. "He was smart enough to get by with robbing a whole community for several weeks! He ought to be able to figure out some way to let us know the Indians had him and his sister."

"Maybe he didn't think anybody would care enough to come looking for them, once you got your horse back," Sarah muttered.

"How would he know I got Willie back?"

"I don't know, Pa, but nobody cared about them before, except Ma and me. The Willards wanted to hang or shoot them!"

"Every man around here, even Willard, rode with us this morning. Every one of us cares, Sary," he said, "or we wouldn't have spent this livelong day hunting for two critters that have given us nothing but trouble since the first day they came to Stoney Creek. Believe me, girl, we all care!"

"But Charlie doesn't know that, Pa," she pointed out. "He probably thinks there's no use leaving a trail that nobody will bother to follow."

Pa dropped his gaze to the floor. "I'm sorry, Sary. I just don't know what else I can do," he said. "Except pray."

"I know, Pa," she said, suddenly sorry she had made him feel bad. "It's just that I have grown so fond of little Katie."

"I'm sorry," he repeated, and he left the cabin.

19

As soon as she entered the classroom the next morning, Sarah noticed a strange odor, something that she knew but couldn't place, something that did not belong in a school or a church.

David looked up at her from the hearth, a puzzled expression on his face. "Didn't I carry in the wood yesterday afternoon, Miss Sarah?" he asked.

"Yes, you did, David," she answered. "You stacked a big pile of it there by the fireplace. Where is it?"

"I don't know! There's a lot of ashes, too, and I know I took out the ashes yesterday just before we left."

She nodded. "Then somebody must have burned our wood during the night. But who could it be?"

Sarah always left the latchstring outside so they could get in each morning. Anyone could have entered the building.

"Do you reckon it was an Injun, Miz Sarah?" Will Junior suggested.

"I don't think so. Indians don't cook bacon." Then she realized that she had put a name to the mysterious odor in the room. It was bacon grease! That's why she had said Indians didn't cook it. She had recognized the scent without realizing it.

"Indians might roast a whole pig or some wild game, but unless they raid somebody's smokehouse, they don't cook bacon. Indians don't kill and process hogs," she explained.

Speaking of raiding a smokehouse reminded her of the side of bacon Charlie had taken from theirs when he and Katie left. Could it be Katie and Charlie staying in the schoolhouse, burning their logs and cooking bacon over the fire? But she refused to get her hopes up over Katie and Charlie.

Perhaps it was Trace, she thought, looking back to where he usually sat and finding his seat empty. Apparently, he had gone out. It had been a real comfort having him here these past few days with all the dangers around them, but the boy was so strange, with his mocking smile and piercing blue eyes, who knew what he might do? He had gone home when they did yesterday, though. Why would he come back and spend the night in the schoolhouse? Had he been trying to set a trap for their wildcat?

"Was Trace home last night, David?" she asked.

"Why, yes, ma'am," David answered with a puzzled look.

"All night?" she pursued.

"I reckon," David said. "He was there when I went to bed, and he ate breakfast with us this morning."

"He was home all night, ma'am," Samuel spoke up. "He sleeps with me, and I had to fight him the whole enduring night for the cover. He just wraps up in it, and it was cold last night!"

If it wasn't Trace, and it wasn't an Indian, who was their

mysterious visitor? Was it just someone seeking shelter from the weather in this conveniently empty building, or did they have something to fear from this intruder?

Sarah didn't want the children out alone today, she decided, but she didn't want to alarm them, either. Then she had an inspiration.

"I think it might be fun to have partners today," she told them. "Samuel, when you go after the water, Will, Junior can go with you. Then, you can help him pass out the tablets. David, Rob can be your partner as you take out the ashes and carry in the wood, and you can help him with the pencils. Jamie, you and Caleb can be a team, and Ruthie, you and I, being the only girls, will join together. Now, let's see how this works as we help each other practice our ABC's."

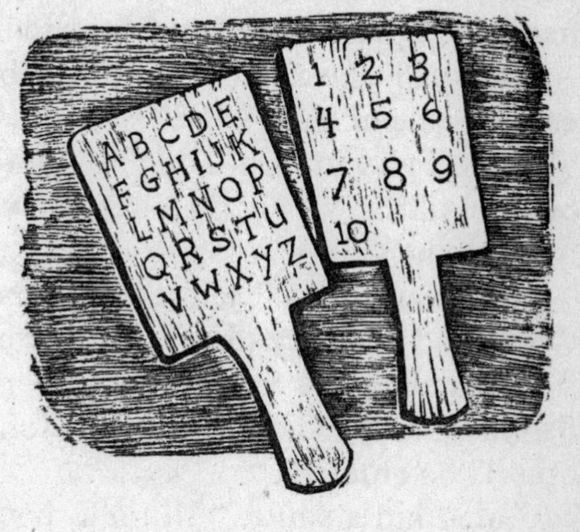

David raised his hand. "Miss Sarah, I need to get in some more wood. I put the last logs on the fire when I built it up just now."

She nodded. "All right, David, but I want Rob to go with you."

Trace came in carrying a full bucket of water. "I didn't want Sammy going down to the spring with that wildcat out there somewhere," he explained.

"Thank you, Trace," Sarah said. "Would you stand guard

while David and Rob bring in some wood? Then bar that door, please." As he got up to do her bidding, she gave a nervous laugh. "I just feel better knowing no one can walk in without knocking first," she explained.

"Wildcats don't knock," Trace informed her with a teasing smile.

"I reckon not, but I'd rather they didn't come in unless I invite them!" she said.

Sarah assigned work according to each pupil's age and ability, and spent the rest of the morning coaching those who needed help. By noon, her fears had begun to fade.

"We will take a quick privy break before we eat our lunches and read our Bible story," she said. "Boys, you go first, and Trace will go with you. I don't think there's anything to fear, but the wildcat was out there yesterday and, as my Pa says, 'It's better to be safe than sorry!'"

"Line up, boys!" Jamie called out. "I'm the Keeper of Order, and you have to line up the way I say. Now, youngest first. Caleb, that's you. Then I go next, followed by you, Sammy, then Rob. Rob and Will Junior, stop pushing each other!" he ordered.

Sarah hid a smile. "All right, boys," she said, "line up, and be quick about getting back inside."

Trace went out first, carrying his gun, and the boys followed. Sarah noticed that the door didn't completely close behind David, but decided to let it go. It wouldn't let in that much cold before they got back.

"Ruthie, help me bring the lunches up by the fire, and we . . ."

She heard the door creak, and surprised that any of the boys would be back so soon, looked up expectantly—straight into the yellow eyes of the biggest wildcat she ever had seen! His ears were laid back, and the hackles on the back of his tawny coat were raised.

"Ruthie, don't make a sound and don't move!" she warned in a low voice that sounded a lot calmer than she felt. "There's a wildcat in the doorway."

Ruthie looked up and screamed, an ear-splitting scream, and the cat shifted his gaze to her.

"Oh, Lord, what am I going to do now?" Sarah prayed.

"Will he eat us?" Ruthie whispered.

Sarah could feel the little girl trembling as she reached over and took her hand. Her own heart was beating against her ribs like a trapped bird.

"Of course, he won't eat us!" she whispered back, not at all sure of that. "My pa says movement attracts wild animals, though. So we will just . . . uh . . . stand here very quietly and wait for Trace to come back with his gun. And we will pray," she added.

The wildcat moved around the door. His yellow eyes searched the room, like a housecat looking for a mouse. Then they came back to fix on Ruthie.

"Miss Sarah, I'm scared!" Ruthie whispered, her voice catching on a sob.

So am I! Sarah thought, but she had to remain calm for Ruthie's sake. She had to think!

The wildcat padded to the middle aisle on silent paws, his eyes still set on Ruthie. His tail began to wag. He bared his teeth, and Sarah heard a growl low in his throat. His yellow eyes flashed fire.

A chill slid down Sarah's spine. *He's ready to attack!* she thought. *And he's aiming for Ruthie!* With those teeth and the claws those huge paws surely hid, he would tear the little girl to shreds. "Dear God, what can I do?" she prayed silently. She looked around for some kind of weapon, but there was none, unless she could grab a stick of wood from the fireplace. If only she were closer to it!

David came through the doorway and stopped. "Whoa!" he breathed, his eyes widening with amazement as he took in the wildcat threatening Ruthie. The other boys bunched up behind him, unable to see into the room. Rob and Will, Junior, into a scuffle as usual, bumped into David, and he fell to his hands and knees. The wildcat whirled to face him.

"Get out, boys!" Sarah called. "It's the wildcat!"

The cat wagged his tail, his eyes fixed on David.

Ruthie began to cry, and Sarah put her arms around her. Then, she saw Trace's head and shoulders appear above the boys' heads.

"Trace, it's the wildcat!" she yelled.

"Get out of here, boys!" Trace ordered, pushing past them into the room, and taking in the big cat now threatening his brother.

"David," he instructed quietly, his pale eyes never leaving the cat, "stay still and don't look him in the eyes. That's a challenge to him, and he will spring."

The wildcat took two steps toward David. He crouched, his tail jerking from side to side.

Sarah saw Trace raise his gun. He motioned for Ruthie and her to get out of the line of fire, and Sarah eased Ruthie toward the corner of the room.

There was a loud crack as the gun went off, and the big cat swayed. He raised one huge paw and swiped at his head. He gave a loud and terrible roar. Then he fell over and lay still.

"Man! Right between the eyes!" Will Junior said from the doorway.

The boys crowded in behind him, staring wide-eyed at the

wild enemy they had feared, now lying still on the schoolroom floor.

"He's a big one, all right!" Rob breathed.

Somehow, the wildcat didn't look so big now, Sarah thought, as he lay there, his front paws crossed at the ankles, his eyes closed.

"Poor kitty!" Jamie said, finally getting past the bigger boys to where he could see.

"Poor kitty?" Will Junior echoed. "That rascal would've eaten you up with one bite, Jamie Moore!"

Samuel and Caleb ran to their brother and helped him up from the floor. David dusted off the knees of his breeches, then moved shakily to the closest bench and sank down on it. "Whew!" he said, holding himself up by propping his hands on his knees.

Sarah sat down quickly on a front bench, her own knees suddenly too weak to hold her. Ruthie, still in her arms, was crying silently. "Thank the good Lord you were here, Trace!" she said. "That cat surely would have mauled at least one of us! How on earth did you manage to hit him with one shot?" She knew she was babbling, but she couldn't seem to stop.

"My gun only holds one shot, ma'am," Trace answered seriously. "If I'd had to reload, David would have been a goner, for sure! I had to hit him the first time."

Sarah joined the rest of them in some excited chatter, then she cleared her throat. "Everyone bring your lunch down here by the fireplace," she said, the teacher again. "Trace, if you will dispose of that cat, we will get on with our lunches and our Bible story."

She read to them while they ate, the story of David hitting the giant Goliath between the eyes with one stone from his slingshot.

"Children," she said then, "let's bow our heads and thank the good Lord for his protection this day."

Sarah led the children in prayer, then decided it was time to close school for the day.

"All right, boys," she said to David and Rob when the prayer was done, "go bring in the wood for tomorrow and take out these ashes. Sammy and Will Junior, take up the wooden paddles and the pencils. We are going home."

They would have been holding school three weeks next Tuesday, Sarah calculated, as she waited for the boys to finish their chores. So far, they had faced bitter cold weather, the threat of Indians, an intruder who spent the night in the classroom, and a wildcat.

Surely there wasn't much else that could threaten them in their little school on Stoney Creek, she thought, as she shut the door behind them and pulled the latchstring through to the outside.

The next morning, Sarah and Jamie hurried along toward the Larkins' under a gray sky that spread over the valley like a heavy woven cover.

She hadn't expected Trace to accompany them to school today, now that the wildcat was dead, but she wasn't sorry to see him. His presence at school yesterday had probably saved at least one of their lives. And they still had the mystery of their nighttime intruder to solve.

"I just thought I would finish out the week," he explained, his eyes on the path ahead of them. "Look at that snow!" Trace said then. "The way the wind's tossing it around, it looks like a new snowstorm!"

"We haven't seen the ground since that first snow fell about the middle of November," Sarah commented. "I've nearly forgotten what grass and dirt look like!"

David ran into the schoolroom ahead of them and went immediately to the fireplace. "Miss Sarah," he called, "this fire couldn't still be burning like this from yesterday! The logs would have been burnt up by now. Anyway, I'm sure I banked it when we left."

"I'm sure you did, too, David," she answered. "Someone must have built it up for us," she said doubt-fully. "Trace, did you stop by here before . . . " But he was shaking his head no.

She said no more, not wanting to frighten the children. She knew their intruder had been here, though. In fact, this fire had been very recently fed. He must have left just before they came into the building.

She couldn't blame anyone for seeking shelter in the empty building, as cold as it was, but who was it? She would not allow herself to hope that it might be Katie and Charlie, though Charlie apparently had taken a side of bacon from Pa's smokehouse, and she definitely had smelled bacon grease in here yesterday.

She didn't smell any bacon grease this morning, though. Either their intruder had run out of bacon, or he had not had time for breakfast before they came.

"Trace, please bar the door and the window shutter," she whispered, as she clapped her hands to get the children's attention. "We will read our Bible story first this morning," she said aloud. "Gather down front around the fireplace and sit close together so we can keep as warm as possible."

By noon, the room still had not warmed up, and Sarah let the children continue to sit around the fireplace as they spread out their lunches. Outside, the wind had begun to moan around the cabin like a hungry wild animal.

"Keep the little ones in here," Trace said. "I'll bring in some more wood."

She nodded. "Thank you, Trace," she said, helping Caleb replace the slab of meat that had slipped out of his biscuit.

★ Chapter Twenty ★

A cold blast of air swept over the room, as Trace unbarred and opened the door.

"Sarah!" he said then. "Look!"

She didn't need to go to the back to see that the outside world was already covered with white, and huge white flakes continued to fall, blown by the wind in a mad swirling pattern that shut out everything but the snow itself.

She ran to the window and opened the shutter, but she couldn't even see the woodpile six feet away.

"Snow!" the Willard boys shouted, racing for the door, with the Mackey brothers right behind them.

Trace barred their way. "You're not going out there, boys," he said firmly. "Not in that blizzard!"

Sarah could feel Ruthie and Jamie pushing against her as they tried to see out the window. She was reminded of that November day the first year they had lived on Stoney Creek, when she had wandered out into a blizzard and been unable to find her way back to the cabin just a few feet away. It had been like walking around under a thick white quilt. If she hadn't heard Ma's voice calling her from the doorway, she might have frozen to death right there in her own front yard!

Panic rose in her throat, but she swallowed it. "What are we going to do, Trace?" she whispered. "How are we going to get these children home?"

"I . . . I'll think of something," he answered. "But, first, we just need to wait and let it quit snowing out there. We can't see now to go anywhere."

Sarah nodded. Why had she ever thought Trace's pale eyes were unnerving? His presence in the schoolhouse was the most comforting thing she could think of right now.

"Let's finish our recitations, boys, Ruthie," Sarah said aloud, making herself calm for the children's sake. "We'll deal with the snow when it's time to go home."

It's time to go home now! her senses cried out, as she listened to the storm howling outside. But she knew Trace was right. They must not venture out in this snowstorm!

Sarah did her best to keep the children busy, but it was all she could do to keep from running to the window and looking out every few minutes herself. She was sure the children felt the same way.

Trace kept his eye on the storm, opening the door a crack and peering out, then turning to shake his head at her. She knew that meant the snow was still coming down. She knew it was still a blizzard by the sound of the wind around the cabin.

"Dear God," she prayed silently, while listening to Rob Willard count to twenty, "Please show us what to do. Please take care of these children. Please stop this storm!" And she prayed it again as she helped Caleb with the first half of the alphabet, and while she helped Jamie and Ruthie practice writing their names.

She glanced at their dwindling pile of logs by the fireplace. What would they do when they were gone? Not even Trace could find his way to the woodpile and back with that howling storm going on out there.

About mid-afternoon, as he threw a big locust log on the fire, David called out, "Miss Sarah, that's the last log! Since I'm Keeper of the Fireplace, do you want me to try to go out and get some more?"

"No, David," she said, wondering what they could do now to keep the fire going. "I know," she said then, "we'll burn our wooden tablets when this log burns down. They're all smeared anyway by now, and Luke can make us some more."

When the time came, the children threw their paddles onto the fire, two at a time to make them last longer. But soon the paddles were all gone, and Sarah looked around for something else to burn. Her gaze fell on the wooden benches, but she didn't know how the people of Stoney Creek would feel about their church pews being destroyed. Still, she was sure they would rather sacrifice the pews than have their children freeze!

"I'm going to try to get to the woodpile," Trace said, peering out the back door again. "The wind has died down, and the snow has nearly stopped, but it's deep. It's piled up against this door halfway to the latch!"

"Surely that's just from drifting, Trace!" Sarah said. "It can't be that deep!"

"Maybe," he answered, "but it's a good thing this door swings inward or we might not be able to get out."

"Can you tell where the woodpile is?" Sarah asked.

"Yeah. It's heaped with snow, but it's still taller than the ground around it. I can see it, if I can just break a path to it."

"Trace, I'm not sure you ought to go out there . . ." she began.

"We've got to have wood, Sarah, or these children will freeze. And I helped my pa make these benches. I don't plan on burning them until the last resort!"

She nodded. "Be careful," she cautioned as he opened the door and a pile of snow fell into the room. Trace shoved his way into the drift.

"I'm thirsty, Miss Sarah," Ruthie said, "and the bucket is empty."

The spring was likely frozen, Sarah realized, even if Samuel could get there. They would have to melt snow for drinking water. But she had nothing to melt it in except the wooden bucket, and it wouldn't do to hang that over the fire! It would be ablaze in no time.

"Samuel, scoop up some of that snow in the water bucket and set it close to the fire. The rest of us will watch Trace carry in wood," she said.

Sarah unbarred the shutter and pulled it back, her nostrils stinging as she drew in a breath of icy air.

"Stand on this bench, and don't lean outside the window," she cautioned the children.

She could see Trace now, rounding the corner of the cabin, plowing into the wall of knee-high snow and making a path through it. Then he was at the woodpile, brushing away snow, working the frozen logs loose from the stack and piling them in his arms until he could hardly see over them. He turned to work his way back through the snow.

Sarah ran to the door, with David and Rob close behind her. Quickly, they unloaded Trace's arms, and he turned back to the woodpile. Before long, most of the wood was inside the schoolroom, stacked all around the fireplace, the melting snow forming puddles on the floor.

Trace shut the door and barred it. He scooped up some snow from the floor and rubbed it on his face and hands. The children watched with puzzled expressions.

"That's to prevent frostbite," he explained, going over to stand by the fire and warm himself.

Sarah sighed in relief. At least they had wood to burn, and the snow in the bucket was beginning to melt a little. They would have water to drink, but if they didn't go home soon, they would need something to eat. If only they could figure out a way to get these children home through snow that was deep enough to reach the littlest ones' waists!

"I could try to make it out to the Larkins'," Trace suggested, as though he had read her thoughts. "Then, I could bring horses back to carry the children home."

★ Chapter Twenty ★

"But it's over a mile to the Larkins', Trace!" she protested. "You'd never make it!"

"If that wind will lay so I can see, I can make it," he insisted.

"All landmarks are covered. Everything out there is white!" she pointed out. "Trace, if you got lost, you'd freeze to death!"

He studied her for several seconds out of those strange, pale eyes. "Do you have a better suggestion?" he asked finally, moving toward the door.

She gave up and walked with him to the back. Removing her scarf from the wooden peg where she had hung it that morning, she wound it around his neck, then handed him her mittens.

"Trace, I don't know what I would have done without you these past days," she said. "You're welcome in my classroom any time."

He reached to unbar the door, then turned back. "Sarah, I wasn't here to make trouble that first day. I . . ." He stopped and looked down at his wet deerskin boots.

"What is it, Trace?" she encouraged.

"I thought I could listen to the lessons and learn how to read and write, without anybody knowing," he blurted. Then his face bright red, he jerked open the door and plunged into the snow.

Sarah stood there speechless for a moment. So that was why he hadn't wanted to read the Bible story to the children the other day! He couldn't read!

"Trace," she called after him, "I'll be glad to teach . . ." She stopped, knowing her words were lost in the moaning of the wind that was rising again.

"I'm hungry, Sarah!" Jamie said. Then there was a chorus of "Me, too!"

"What are we going to do, Miss Sarah, if Trace doesn't come back?" Will Junior asked.

"My brother will be back!" David shouted. "Trace always keeps his word!"

"Will means if he gets lost and doesn't get back soon," Sarah soothed. "But Trace knows what he's doing, and God will help him. He'll get through," she said, wishing she was as sure of that as she sounded.

"Let's say a prayer for Trace," Sarah said. "I know God will protect him."

The wind mocked her shaky faith. She opened the window a crack and peered out. It was snowing again, as thickly and as wildly as before.

"Oh, Lord," she prayed fervently and silently, "if You don't help him, Trace hasn't got a chance!"

Sarah shut and barred the window, then turned to the class. "Everybody take a small drink of melted snow, so we can start melting another bucketful. If there's anything we have plenty of, it's snow!" she said, laughing. The children looked back at her solemnly.

"I'm so hungry, my stomach hurts, Sarah!" Jamie wailed. "Haven't you got *anything* to eat?"

"I'm sorry, Jamie. We ate the sausage and biscuits I brought for our lunch. Does anybody have any food left?" she asked.

"I have a piece of cornbread and half an onion," Rob Willard volunteered.

"I've got a piece of cornbread, too," Ruthie said.

"I've got a cold potato," Samuel Mackey added.

"That's wonderful!" Sarah exclaimed with sudden inspiration. "We can make a pot of soup!" She looked around the room. "If we had something to cook it in," she added, her excitement dying as she realized there was nothing. If she ever taught another school, she vowed, she would stock her classroom with all kinds of utensils and supplies!

"I've heard my pa talk about making soup in a turtle shell once when he was out on the trail," Will Junior said.

"That's clever," Sarah answered. "Our problem is, we don't have a turtle shell." *Or anything else,* she thought despondently. One potato and one onion wouldn't go very far among so many, even if she didn't eat, but a good, hot pot of soup would have given all of them some nourishment and eased the pangs of hunger for a while.

The wind hurled itself at the cabin, its moaning almost like that of a human being. Sarah shivered, wondering where Trace was now. Had he made it to the Larkins' place yet? Was he lost out there in this terrible, freezing whiteness?

Suddenly, beneath the wind's endless crying, she thought she heard another sound. Quickly, she opened the shutter and peered out into the whirling snow. There it was again! A human cry for help! She was sure of it.

Sarah shut the window and ran to the door, thinking that Trace must have come back. Maybe he was hurt, or nearly frozen! She flung open the door, but there was nothing out there except the wind and the snow. Both came in with a vengeance until she slammed the door shut.

Surely she had imagined the faint cry for help, she told herself, walking back to the front of the room and picking up Pa's Bible. She would read the children another story to keep their minds off their troubles. She leafed through the pages. Maybe the story of the little boy who shared his lunch with Jesus would be appropriate, but she didn't want to mention food just now.

"Help!" The faint cry seemed to come right out of the fireplace. Nonsense! Sarah scolded herself. It must have been her imagination.

★ Chapter Twenty-One ★

"What was that, Miss Sarah?" Ruthie asked. "I thought I heard somebody call for help."

All right, she thought, *it wasn't my imagination.* She took her cloak from its wooden peg and threw it around her. "I'm going outside for a few minutes. Keep the door and the window shut, and practice reciting the alphabet," she told the children. "I'll be right back."

Sarah unbarred the door, and the wind snatched it out of her hands and flung it against the wall. She saw David and Samuel running to shut it as she plunged into the snow. It was above her knees, and in seconds her moccasins and stockings were soaked. The cold air stung her nostrils and scraped its way into her lungs. Already, her body had begun to shake under her heavy cloak.

She felt her way around the building by sliding her hand along its bark-covered logs. Without the church wall to guide her, she could wander into the blinding fury of wind and snow and never find her way back. They would find her there, frozen solid, when the snow melted, she thought grimly, edging around the back corner of the building.

Sarah could see nothing except snow, falling from the sky, whirling in the wind, covering everything, drifting against the cabin and its wide stone chimney.

She gasped and stepped back. Had that big drift by the chimney moved? Suddenly she remembered the wildcat Trace had killed yesterday. Was there a second wildcat that had taken shelter near the warmth of the chimney?

"Wildcats don't ask for help!" she told herself aloud, brushing at the drift. Soon she uncovered the near-frozen form of a child huddled beneath the snow!

Keeping close to the cabin wall, Sarah carried the shivering child back to the door and kicked against it. "Let me in!"

she called. "Hurry!"

The door swung open, with David and Rob behind it, and she stumbled into the cabin. She heard them shut and bar it behind her.

"It's a person!" David said in amazement.

"Is it dead?" Rob asked.

"Not quite," Sarah panted, laying her burden as near the fire as she could. "Boys, bring me some snow!" she ordered, stripping away the tattered remains of a cover the child had wrapped around itself. Underneath was a familiar brown dress.

"Katie?" Sarah whispered. "Katie, is it you?"

The child moaned and began to shiver violently.

"Where's Charlie?" Sarah asked.

The wind moaned around the chimney. "Katie!" it seemed to call. "Katie!" Or was it the wind?

Sarah went to the door and opened it. At first, all she saw was snow. Then a huge, dark shape came around the cabin. It was a horse and rider!

"Trace?" she called. Oh, thank God, he had made it!

The rider slid to the ground and came toward her. "Where's Katie?" he demanded.

"Charlie!" she gasped. "Come in. Katie's here, up by the fireplace. She was nearly frozen when I found her!"

He tied the horse to a snow-covered tree branch and came into the schoolroom, stamping snow from his wet moccasins. He threw off what appeared to be the other half of Katie's ragged cover, and strode to the bench where his little sister lay.

"Kate?" he said softly. "Kate, it's me, Charlie. I got a horse and came back for you, just like I said I would."

The little girl did not open her eyes or make a sound.

Sarah grabbed some snow and rubbed it on her face and hands. Again, she warmed her cloak by the fire, then wrapped it around the child.

If only Ma were here! she thought desperately. *I don't know what else to do!*

"If we had that soup," Samuel said wistfully, "that would warm her up inside. Ma always gives us hot soup when we get chilled."

"I told you I don't have anything to make soup in!" Sarah snapped. The boy flinched as though she had hit him. "Oh, Sammy," she apologized, "I'm sorry! I'm just upset about Katie and about you all not having anything to eat. I didn't mean to hurt your feelings."

"It's all right, Miss Sarah," he said, taking a seat on the bench behind Katie.

"Have you got something to make soup with?" Charlie asked. "I've got a tin basin in my pack."

"We've got an onion and a potato," Sarah said eagerly.

"We might have a potato or two left, but we ran out of meat yesterday," Charlie said.

"Bacon," Sarah guessed. "You and Katie have been staying here at night, haven't you?"

He nodded. "We were afraid to go back to the cave, now that everybody knows where it is. We just camped out as long as we could, then I remembered that this building was empty at night."

"Charlie, all we've ever wanted to do is help you and Katie. Why didn't you just stay in the church today?" she asked. "Katie wouldn't have been exposed to that freezing weather if you had."

He looked at his feet. "I thought she'd be all right there against the chimney with the heat from the fire inside, until I could get back with some food for tonight and you all left."

"Where did you get the horse?" she questioned.

"I didn't steal it, if that's what you mean." His dark eyes met hers squarely. "I haven't stolen anything since we left your place. We took some supplies with us then, but we left the brooch to pay for them. It's worth a lot of money."

Sarah nodded. "But where did you get the horse?"

"The old man in the cabin over the hill let me borrow it, the one with the funny way of talking. They didn't give us food because he and his wife want me to bring Katie back there, but I think they want us to stay with them, and I don't . . ."

Sarah sighed. "Charlie, you and Katie need a family, and the Strausbergs have always wanted children. You've got to learn to accept the help God sends you."

His eyes met hers for what seemed like a long time. She could see questions in them, but she didn't find the mockery she had seen there the last time she had talked with him about God.

"I'll get the basin and potatoes," he said finally.

As he went out, Sarah could see that the snow had stopped, and she could barely hear the wind now around the corners of the cabin. The sky had darkened some. Before long, it would be night.

Katie moaned and stirred under the heavy cloak. She opened her eyes. "Charlie?" she called weakly.

Sarah ran to her. "It's Sarah, Katie, and Charlie's here."

Katie tried to sit up. "My feet are asleep," she complained.

Charlie threw the basin and potatoes down on the bench. He jerked off Katie's frozen moccasins and stockings. Her feet were blue with cold, and he rubbed them with snow, then began to massage them. Katie moaned with pain as feeling began to return.

"Walk on them!" Charlie ordered, and groaning, Katie obeyed, stumbling back and forth before the fireplace, holding tightly to her brother's arm.

Sarah filled the basin with melted snow, and picked up the potatoes Charlie had brought. Charlie handed her his hunting knife, and she quickly sliced the potatoes, peelings and all, into the water. Then she added Samuel's potato and Rob's onion.

"Don't put that log on yet," she warned David, who was heading for the fireplace with a maple chunk in his hands. "That low, hot fire is just right for cooking. We can build up the fire when our soup is done."

"Well, it needs salt, but it's better than nothing," Jamie declared a while later as he finished his dipperful of the hot, thin liquid with the leftover cornbread crumbled into it.

"You sound just like Pa!" Sarah laughed, feeling better now that they at least had something in their stomachs. Katie was looking better by the minute since she had swallowed her share of soup. Before morning, though, these children would be hungry again, and Sarah had absolutely nothing else to feed them.

"Miss Sarah, are we going to have to stay here all night?" Caleb asked plaintively.

"Well, Caleb, I don't know," she began.

Ruthie's blue eyes filled with tears. "I want my ma!" she wailed. Sarah went to put her arm around the little girl.

"I could take 'em home two at a time on the horse," Charlie volunteered.

"Listen!" Sarah said. "I thought I heard horses!" She flew to the door and pulled it open as several dark shapes rode into the yard.

"Are you ready to close school now, Sary girl?" Pa asked from Willie's broad back. Sarah knew, if she could see him, he would be wearing a teasing smile, but all she could do was cry.

22

Sarah looked around the familiar church building. She had not been in it since that awful day in November when the first winter blizzard had marooned her there with her seven pupils.

It had been the hardest winter imaginable, with many heavy snows that had covered the ground until the middle of February, and it had been too cold to go to church. Sarah's family had had all they could do to survive, and even with two fireplaces, their cabin had never been completely warm. Cattle had frozen in their pens and wild game froze in the forest. Even some settlers, they had heard, had died from the cold. Others had headed back East as soon as the weather permitted, vowing never to return to such a place.

Everybody on Stoney Creek had survived, though, and none of them had given up. There sat the Larkins, little Ruthie waving at Jamie across the aisle. There were the Mackeys with their new baby, Joshua. And there were the red-haired Willards, Rob and Will Junior sitting with their pa, and pretty, green-eyed Rachel sitting with her ma. Sarah saw her turn and wink at somebody behind them. She looked back just in time to see Trace Mackey return the wink. Then he winked at Sarah, too, and she whirled around, her face hot with embarrassment.

Sarah never would forget Trace saving them from the wildcat, though, or his volunteering to go for help the day of the blizzard. If Pa, Luke, Mark Larkin, and Mr. Mackey hadn't set out to rescue their children and come across him wandering around lost in the blinding snow, he would have frozen to death within shouting distance of the Larkins' cabin.

He obviously was all right now, she thought, vowing she would not make the mistake of looking his way again this morning. She would teach him to read and write, though, if it were the last thing she did! She felt she owed him that much.

Sarah's gaze fell on Katie, wearing a pretty new yellow dress with her beautiful brooch pinned at the neck, and leaning contentedly against Mrs. Strausberg, who had her arm around the little girl. Charlie sat across the way beside Mr. Strausberg, his dark eyes taking in everything and giving back nothing of his own thoughts. *Maybe Jeremy Justice would have something special to say just for Charlie this morning,* she thought hopefully. God often worked in mysterious ways.

"Good morning!" the preacher said, his long strides carrying him quickly to the front of the room. "Isn't it good to be here this bright March morning?"

There was a fervid chorus of Amens and Mr. Mackey called out, "It's just plain good to have survived the winter!" There was scattered laughter mingled with another chorus of amens.

"God is good, brothers and sisters," the preacher said. "I

know He certainly has been good to me and, now that the winter weather surely is behind us, I plan to be with you to tell you about Him every fourth Sunday."

He nodded at Mr. Mackey, who called out, "Oh, God, our help in ages past, our strength in days to come!" The congregation sang the line and waited for him to call out another.

"Our shelter from the stormy blast, and our eternal home!" he lined, and they sang.

Sarah felt joy flood through her. The shadows that had fallen on Stoney Creek this past year had melted away in the warm spring sunshine, and there was much for which to be thankful.

Soon she would open her spring school in the new, one-room log cabin Pa and the other men were building in sight of the Moore cabin. She and her pupils would never have to fear being alone with Indians, wildcats, or blizzards again.

Luke's new cabin was finished and waiting for Betsy and him to move in after the wedding. Ma and Mrs. Larkin were busy making another quilt.

Pa and Mark Larkin had gone to Harrodstown to replenish supplies for all the families, and had talked a new family into moving to Stoney Creek, the Hudsons and their three children. Mr. Hudson was staying with the Strausbergs while the men helped him build a cabin up past the Willards'. Then his wife and children would come on over from the fort.

"Before I begin my message this morning, I have a couple of announcements," the preacher said. "You all are invited to witness the exchanging of marriage vows between Miss Betsy Larkin and Mr. Luke Moore immediately following the service here on the fourth Sunday of April."

That was no news, Sarah thought with amusement. Everybody on Stoney Creek knew Luke and Betsy were getting married next month, and each family had promised to contribute some item of household plunder for the new home. Sarah would be standing up with Betsy, wearing her green silk dress Aunt Charity had made her to wear to the Governor's Ball, the one the preacher said exactly matched her eyes.

"Also, I want you to know that I am planning to build a cabin over beyond the Strausbergs, and I have sent back East for the merchandise to stock a small store," Jeremy Justice continued. "I won't be here all the time, of course, with my preaching duties elsewhere, but if you need something from the store when I'm away, you can contact Mrs. Strausberg, and she will see that you get it."

A little village was growing up on the banks of Stoney Creek, Sarah thought, just as Pa had predicted. Pa had the mill. Mr. Willard had become the neighborhood blacksmith, shoeing their horses and making nails and tools. Mr. Strausberg, who had been a skilled woodcarver back in Germany, had offered to make furniture for those who wanted it. Mr. Mackey helped with whatever the others needed, trading work for services.

It wasn't Williamsburg, Virginia. It wasn't even Miller's Forks. But it was a far cry from the lonely wilderness Sarah and her family had endured that first year when Pa had brought them, against her wishes, to the banks of Stoney Creek.

"Life sometimes just grabs us and drags us down first one rough road and then another, bumping and bruising, thwarting all our plans to stroll leisurely down some other path entirely," Jeremy Justice broke into her thoughts. "Sometimes it seems that we are so busy coping with what life brings, that we never have time to do the things we wanted to do, to go the places we meant to go.

"My text this morning is taken from Proverbs 3: 5, 6."

The words of the familiar verses went through Sarah's

★ Chapter Twenty-Two ★

mind before he could read them: "Trust in the Lord with all thine heart; and lean not unto thine own understanding. In all thy ways acknowledge Him, and He shall direct thy paths."

"It is the journey, itself, that is important," the preacher was saying. "God teaches us through the disappointments, the frustrations, the tragedies that we encounter along the way, how to be the kind of people He wants to spend eternity with Him."

He looked at Mrs. Strausberg sitting with Katie, and then at Mr. Strausberg with Charlie. "The Strausbergs, here, are the perfect example," he said. "This couple buried each of the children they brought into this world, but they did not let their journey down that hard path embitter them. They trusted in the Lord, and today He has rewarded them with a family."

Sarah felt a glow of happiness spread through her. She was glad that Charlie had decided he and Katie would stay with the Strausbergs. They had all gone through such hard times in the past, and now it was working out so well for them.

How would things work out for her? She would be fifteen soon. Even rougher than the road she had traveled through the wilderness to reach Kentucky was the road she had traveled toward growing up since then. Where would her journey take her before it was finished?

Sarah had found the promise of those verses in Proverbs to be true, though. The Lord was always there to direct her paths when she trusted Him to do it.

Sarah sighed contentedly. With God to direct her paths, she decided as she settled down to listen to Jeremy Justice's message, she could just sit back and enjoy the rest of the journey.

Then she smiled. *Beginning with today,* she thought, for the preacher was going home with the Hiram Moore family for dinner.

Echoes from the Past

For some of the rough frontiersmen, religion was part of the civilization they had eagerly left behind them. But many of the Kentucky settlers, like Sarah Moore's pa, depended upon strong faith in God to help them survive the dangers and hardships they faced.

The first preaching service in Kentucky was held on Sunday, May 28, 1775. That day, under the shade of a huge elm tree at Boonesborough, the Reverend John Lythe of the Church of England gave the sermon. In May of 1776, a similar service was held at Harrodstown by the Reverend Peter Tinsley, a Baptist. These denominations were soon followed by the Presbyterians, the Methodists, and the Catholics.

As soon as most settlers had roofs over their heads, they began to build a place for worship, much like the one Sarah attended on Stoney Creek. One of the most unusual of these was Old Mulkey Meeting House, originally built around 1798 by Phillip Mulkey and a group of Baptists from North and

South Carolina. The first cabin soon became too small and was replaced by a building of half-hewn, chinked logs, built in the shape of a cross. It had twelve corners, believed to represent the twelve Apostles, and three doors to represent the Holy Trinity. This building may still be seen near Tompkinsville, Kentucky.

In June of 1800, the Reverend James McGready, a Presbyterian, led an evangelistic meeting at Red River Meeting House, near Russellville, that began Kentucky's "Great Revival." Practical frontiersmen had little patience with long-winded discussions of theology. Reverend McGready "told it like it was," and his preaching attracted hundreds to the little church. In fact, people came from such great distances that they found it necessary to camp overnight at the meeting place. The "camp meeting" was born.

In August of 1801, when Sarah was an "old lady" of thirty-six years, 25,000 people flocked to the little log Cane Ridge Meeting House to hear eighteen Presbyterian preachers, and at least that many Methodists and Baptists. The Great Revival swept through Kentucky like a forest fire, and fundamentalism took root in the ashes of the old formal religions.

The fundamentalists simply believed that each individual can gain eternal life and have a personal relationship with God by confessing that he or she is a sinner in need of the salvation provided by the death of His Son, Jesus Christ. They built their doctrine around John 3:16 from the Bible, which states: "God so loved the world that He gave His only Son, that whosoever believes in Him should not perish, but have everlasting life."

Many church groups split, with each division joining others who believed as they did, forming new congregations. For example, Reverend Barton Stone left the Presbyterians to

found the Christian Church, and later joined Alexander Campbell to form the denomination known today as Disciples of Christ. The Church of Christ grew out of another division of that group.

In the early 1900's, the fundamentalists and the more formal religions were joined first by the pentecostals and then by the charismatics. Both groups held the basic beliefs of the fundamentalists, with the added teaching that the miracles recorded in the Book of Acts are available to Christians at all times. Congregations representing all of these beliefs—and others—are alive and well in Kentucky today.

A religion that did not fare so well over time was perhaps the most unusual to ever come to Kentucky. The Shakers were a group who held some different ideas from most of the mainstream churches of the day. They believed in communal living, where they ran their own schools for the children and made all their own food, clothing, and household items.

The Shakers crafted pewter dishes and utensils, and created furniture of a simple, classic design that is still in demand today. They invented the clothespin, the modern flat broom, water-repellant fabric, and many labor-saving tools. A Shaker woman, inspired by her spinning wheel, developed the water-powered circular saw. Her invention revolutionized the lumber industry. Shaker salesmen traveling Kentucky roads and rivers found many customers eager to buy their crafts, garden seed, and livestock. Shakers were known to be honest tradesmen and sell goods of the highest quality.

The Pleasant Hill village, one of the Shaker communities, had almost 500 members at its peak in the 1830's. The community thrived for about fifty years until the Civil War came to Kentucky. Both the Union and Confederate armies took huge amounts of Shaker food and horses as they traveled

through the countryside to different battlegrounds. The Shakers never recovered from these losses. Also, their dedicated leaders were growing old and dying, and most Shaker children left the communities by the time they were eighteen. By 1910 the Pleasant Hill Community had ceased to exist.

Kentucky's first school was taught in 1775 by Mrs. William Coomes in the little one-room, dirt-floored log building that Sarah visited on her first trip to the fort at Harrodstown. There was no chinking between the logs, but the room had a huge stone fireplace, and the windows were covered with paper greased with bear fat, which let in some light while keeping out the wind. The children sat on rough, backless, half-log benches and wrote on wooden paddles with sticks blackened in the fire, much as they did in Sarah's school on Stoney Creek. Reading, writing, and simple arithmetic were taught from paddles showing numerals and the alphabet. Their only "textbook" was the Bible.

As far as is known, the first school in Kentucky, at Boonesborough, was taught by Joseph Doniphan in the summer of 1779. Soon most settlements had schools much like the one at Fort Harrod—for the boys. Except for Sarah's little school, there is no record that girls attended school in Kentucky until the early 1800's. With such comforts as desks, stoves, glass windows, and wooden floors added, the one-room school remained a part of Kentucky life for many years.

The first college west of the Allegheny Mountains was Transylvania College, founded in 1780 in Lexington, when what is now Kentucky's second-largest city was just one year old. Today, Kentucky has many accredited universities and colleges.

With multi-million dollar buildings housing Kentucky's schools today, and with Kentucky teams competing at state,

national, and world levels in every sport from checkers to basketball, it is hard to imagine it all began in a one-room, dirt-floored log cabin, with homemade games at "recess" on the hard-packed dirt of a schoolyard.

Where did Sarah Moore fit into all this growth of religion and education? Did she continue to teach her little school on the banks of Stoney Creek? Did she marry the preacher and work with him to build up the church there, or travel with him to some other growing congregation? Did she instead marry Trace Mackey or Katie's brother, Charlie, or some new Stoney Creek resident she had yet to meet? Did she have children of her own? Did she seek new religious experiences as an adult during the Great Revival?

Whatever roads she traveled, you can be sure that Sarah was deeply involved in the affairs of her family and community all the days of her life, continually desiring to let God direct her paths.